Dead Man's Canyon

DEAD MAN'S CANYON

JACKSON COLE

WHEELER
CHIVERS

This Large Print edition is published by Wheeler Publishing, Waterville, Maine, USA and by AudioGO Ltd, Bath, England.
Wheeler Publishing, a part of Gale, Cengage Learning.
The text of this Large Print edition is unabridged.
Other aspects of the book may vary from the original edition.
Set in 16 pt. Plantin.

LIBRARY OF CONGRESS CATALOGING-IN-PUBLICATION DATA

Cole, Jackson.
    Dead man's canyon / by Jackson Cole.
        p. cm. — (Wheeler Publishing large print Western)
    ISBN-13: 978-1-4104-3487-6 (softcover)
    ISBN-10: 1-4104-3487-7 (softcover)
    1. Large type books. I. Title.
PS3505.O2685D39 2011
813'.52—dc22   2010045636

BRITISH LIBRARY CATALOGUING-IN-PUBLICATION DATA AVAILABLE
Published in 2011 in the U.S. by arrangement with Golden West Literary Agency.
Published in 2011 in the U.K. by arrangement with Golden West Literary Agency.

U.K. Hardcover: 978 1 445 83640 9 (Chivers Large Print)
U.K. Softcover: 978 1 445 83641 6 (Camden Large Print)

Printed in the United States of America
1 2 3 4 5 6 7 15 14 13 12 11

DEAD MAN'S CANYON

CHAPTER I
DEATH RAID

The hot wind swirled across the tremendous expanse of southwest Texas. Whistling down from mountain peaks into the narrow canyons of rivers, it rustled dry pods of mesquite, cleaning layers of dust from the arms of giant cactus growths. Before it scudded black clouds that cast shadows as they moved high above the earth, darkening the waist-deep grass in the stream bottom.

The Slash E was a good-sized outfit. It touched the Pecos on the east, its cows ranging all over the first-grade fodder to the rim of Brewster County.

Brewster, land of innumerable range mysteries, once was the stamping grounds and hereditary road south for the Comanche raiders from the Staked Plain. It occupied hundreds of square miles of brush-choked mountain country and was now favored by the lawless as a refuge from the righteous vengeance of their fellow-men. Unexplored in many regions, Brewster swung its big bend deep into Mexico with the curve of the Rio Grande. For long distances malpais cliffs shut in the river — cracked, bad volcanic country on which a man could not walk far and no animal's hoofs could find purchase.

As the breeze swirled and puffed into a canyon door, it blew to glowing life the coals of a wood-fire, built against a cliff so the heat reflected back. A six-foot-long object stirred in a rolled khaki blanket in this warmth. Pete Norris returned suddenly to consciousness.

"Ugh!" the cowboy grunted.

He opened sun-seamed brown eyes in the moonlight, listened to catch the sound that must have disturbed him. He heard only the familiar movements of animals, horses in lasso corral, penned steers up the draw, which Norris had ridden so far to drive back closer to Slash E range. Those sounds would never startle him out of a deep sleep.

Half a dozen of his waddies snored about him, range riders who took Norris' orders. For though short on years — not much past twenty — Pete was long in headwork and a skilled range rider, bronc buster and steer handler. He was a foreman and the boss back home had intrusted him with responsible tasks before.

Norris prided himself on always carrying out instructions to the letter, his ability to make money for his brand, and being able to work twenty-four hours a day if need be, for the Slash E. Every self-respecting cowboy felt the same.

He had been using his wide, brown, flat-crowned Nebraska hat as a pillow for his curly, short-cut head. In the moonlight, the firm line of Pete's bronzed jaw could be seen. His even features were set as he listened. He still wore his blue levis and shirt. His chaps were near at hand, by his spurred boots. Those were the only articles he had removed for comfort while sleeping.

The Slash E steers Norris and his men were turning back home browsed a short way up the barranca. They could not escape past the lariats stretched from rock to rock at the constricted mouth. There were several hundred of them, truculent from a year's wandering in the wilds.

Abruptly the absolute peace of the Texas night was shattered by gunshots, demoniacal shrieks that slashed back and forth between the steep red-rock walls. Pete Norris dived for the six-shooter in its holster belt, never far from a cowboy's hand.

"Up, boys!" he roared. "Rustlers!"

He had guessed right the first instant. Hard-riding hombres, their guns marked by blue-yellow flashes stabbing the night, spurred in on the handful of cowboys.

Norris' six-gun cocked under his thumb. He threw a bullet at the shadowy attackers, grunted with satisfaction as he heard a man screech. A mustang swerved from the gang, its rider slumped over the horn. His men leaped awake. Pistols in calloused hands even as their eyes opened, they were ready to fight for their lives to guard their employer's property.

"To the rocks, pronto!" shouted Pete.

His quick eye took in the fact that they were outnumbered eight or ten to one. The fierce attackers were flooding down on them like the roaring crest of a swollen river. Colts seemed everywhere, aimed their way. The gang, Norris knew, must have spied them from a distance in the day, marked their camp, then come to strike in the night.

Acrid powdersmoke mingled chokingly with the dust from beating, sliding hoofs. Norris glimpsed the big chief of the gang. The light was dim, but the leader swung his great black stallion around so the ruby fire struck his face.

Though he was masked to the long nose, the flashing eyes were visible, and bristling red hair hung from beneath his Stetson. His body was big as a hogshead, but despite his size, he handled his wild horse with a centaur's ease. A vest flapped loose at his burly hips, where thick brown-leather chaps were bunched. His booted feet were thrust into tapped stirrups. One hand held the reins to guide the stallion, the other a flaming revolver.

"Wipe 'em out!" he bawled, his voice harshly deep.

Pete Norris kept swiftly shooting back at them as he scuttled for cover behind some broken rocks up the barranca. He noted a thin Mexican in velvet pants, sash and fancy vest, peaked sombrero dotted with white buttons. From under the curved hat brim came the glint of fierce dark eyes. The skin of the forehead was olive over the bandanna mask.

There were too many more for him to memorize. Two of his boys had been hit with lead in the first awful volley. They lay silent in death, cowboys who had met a violent, unlucky end. A third was dragging a broken leg behind him as he sought to reach the boulders. Norris leaped back to assist him, Colt snarling defiance at the driving killers. The giant leader swerved to pour slugs into the spine of the wounded

11

waddy, finishing him off.

"Damn yore dirty heart and soul!" yelled Norris, teeth gritting.

He let go a snap-shot at the giant chief as the hombre jerked reins. He had the grim satisfaction of seeing the murderer jump in his leather, hearing the curses of pain.

Then a couple of dozen guns swung Pete Norris' way. He was aware of a stunning, blasting volley as he stumbled on the loose shale. It seemed aimed right at his eyes, and total blackness smote him as he went down with pole-axed finality.

Deep in the wild, rugged Brewster mountains the following night, eighty miles from the spot where Pete Norris and his unfortunate crew had been gunned, the big rustler chief, trailed by his Mex crony and half a dozen outlaw horsemen, rode into a hidden camp. They passed through the gate, formed by natural rock cliffs, and came into a shallow, flattened basin that was screened by thick bush.

Several tough-looking fellows slouched about fires built in the shelter of red cliffs that broke the smoke columns in the day and shut off any glow at dark. Eastward, over a low shoulder, the land dropped into a narrow valley, with towering, forbidding mountains blocking the way east, effectively shutting off this section. The valley, through which ran a crooked creek, was choked with brush and high, luscious grass. From it came the lowing of steers.

"Red Frankie" Guire, chief of the gun-slinging cattle thieves, had dropped the bandanna mask which had concealed his features during the brutal attack on Pete Norris' camp. He was sweaty and dust-covered from the long, fast ride which had brought him back to headquarters. A blood-stained bandage showed through a tear in his shirt, where Pete's bullet had nipped his flesh.

Guire swung stiffly from saddle, slouched toward the central fire. The men who awaited him there looked up inquiringly as he came in. In the firelight, Guire's features showed plainly. He had a bulldog jaw bristling with red whiskers that matched his thatch of hair. His lips were sullenly thick, his greenish-hued eyes slitted. A tobacco cud distorted his leathery, florid cheek, and his nose was long and predatory. His hands were like frying-pans at the ends of his great arms. His shoulders were slumped, his legs bowed to a horse's ribs.

"Gimme a drink," he snarled, snatching a whisky bottle and putting it to his lips.

Red Guire was a killer and expert gunman. He had rustled cows from the Canadian border to the ranchos of old Mexico. He knew every cunning trick of the rewrite men — how to switch a brand, disguise it so that even the calf's own mother wouldn't know it. Shaggy, hirsute growth showed at the open V of his shirt. Under his bandanna, his head sat almost squarely on his great shoulders, for he had scarcely any neck. His Colts had black handles, smoothed from constant use, worn reversed.

"What in tarnation hit yuh, Guire?" demanded the hombre beside whom the redhead squatted.

Guire had practically drained the half-empty bottle. He smacked his lips, wiped his mouth with the back of his dirty arm.

"Aw, we seen a good bunch of Slash E stuff, and come up on the waddies drivin' 'em, Boss," said Guire surlily. "One pinked me across the ribs, but it tickled more'n hurt. Francisco and me rode over ahead. The boys 're runnin' the steers in the usual way, fast and smooth."

Francisco de Lira, Guire's Mex shadow and knifeman, sat by his huge pard. His high-peaked sombrero was trimmed with rows of pearl buttons. His body was lithe as a rattler's, but he was much more danger-

14

ous than his reptilian counterpart. The long-bladed fang he wielded was directed by a sinister human brain. The skin of his face was smooth and olive, the eyes like buttons, the patent-leather hair plastered to his narrow head.

The curve of his thin lips was cruel as a falcon's beak, a penciled, close-clipped black mustache making it seem still narrower.

The chiefs squatted, heads almost together, in the circle. The hombre even Guire called "Boss" said authoritatively:

"Atchinson's got to die. He's in the way and I won't have any man stoppin' me, just as I've got things rollin'." His voice was low and murderous, vitriolic hate dripping from it. He seemed furious at life and decency. "Cows're comin' in from as far off as Oklahoma. The market's high. But it all depends on how quiet we hold it over here. We'll keep guards out day and night. But don't forget that Atchinson must be taken care of at once."

"You weesh me to keel Atchinson, Senor Mohle?" breathed de Lira.

He patted his pants legs. There rode his sheathed stiletto, more dangerous and far quieter than a gun at close range.

"We'll figure it carefully, so as not to be

15

suspected —" began Mohle.

His eyes glowed with feral ferocity in the firelight. He broke off, for there was a stir at the gate. Mohle swung, hand dropping to the Colt strapped about his waist. He stepped back into the black shadows of the cliff, while his men tensed, ready for trouble.

An hombre in cowboy garb, flogging a chestnut mustang flecked with lather, rode into the rustler stronghold. His face was red, sweated under the dark Stetson. Flinging himself from his saddle, he cried:

"Howdy, boys! Listen, Atchinson's comin'. I couldn't turn him this time. He's been growin' more and more careful, and he's on the prod."

"How many with him?" growled Red Guire.

"Four waddies, besides me. I managed to cut over him, ahead of 'em."

CHAPTER II
DEATH AND RETURN

Mohle, the gang boss, snapped some orders. Guire's bull voice relayed them to the rustlers in camp. They hid themselves, only the handful with Mohle remaining in sight. A messenger leaped on a bronc and rode down the valley, to fetch up reinforcements.

Half an hour later, a big, gray-haired Texan, trailed by a quartet of cowboys, came slowly through the gate into the camp. Huge of body, with crisp, iron-gray mustache and a strong face, was "Pop" Atchinson, owner of the Circle 3. He held a Winchester carbine short in his hands as he approached the silent group that included Guire and de Lira.

"Howdy," growled the rancher, eying them with suspicion.

He did not dismount, but sat his leather.

"Huh," grunted Guire. "What yuh ride into my camp at night for, feller?"

Pop Atchinson scowled. "Mebbe it's yore camp, Sorrel-top, but it's on my range." He paused and the wind carried to his alert ears the bawling of cattle. As he sniffed, his light-blue eyes slitted. "Brandin' at night. I've come up with yuh, I reckon. You devils, yuh've stripped me bare of beef, me'n the whole county! But now —"

"But now what, Atchinson?"

It was the boss, Mohle, speaking from the shadows. The old rancher swung, peering his way.

"Who's that?" he demanded.

"Mohle."

"Mohle?" Atchinson's face twisted into a deep scowl. "King of the Rustlers!"

17

"So you remember, eh? Always were clever trailin' rustlers, weren't you, Atchinson?" The boss was taunting, some long-nurtured hate shaking his sinister voice. "Couldn't let you die without remindin' you of the necktie party you staged, you and your pals."

"Mohle's dead! We strung him higher'n a kite. Switchin' brands, he deserved it —"

Atchinson broke off as he suddenly understood the trap. He sensed the presence of many gunnies softly closing in about the exits, cutting them off from escape. Such a man never knew fear, but he was a wary fighter.

"Shoot it out, boys!" roared Pop Atchinson.

Jerking his reins, he yanked up his Winchester.

"Give it to 'em!" bellowed Mohle.

Atchinson fired, a long bullet ripping a hole in de Lira's high-peaked Stetson. The Mexican had whipped his knife out with magic speed. He sprang in to grasp the reins to prevent Atchinson's escape.

But Mohle, Colt leaping to view, let go an instant later. The slug caught Atchinson in the cheek, tore up through the roof of his mouth and blasted into his brain, killing him instantly.

At the same moment roared a volley from

rustler guns, and a couple of snap-shots from Atchinson's waddies. But it was over before Atchinson hit the ground. Writhing, dying mustangs were down, pinning beneath them their bullet-pierced riders. The Circle 3 owner and his men stiffened in death on the blood-stained earth.

Mohle, nostrils flared, big Colt gripped in hand, stepped out and checked up on the bodies. One was still alive. Mohle put a finishing shot into the man's head.

"Bury the horses," Mohle commanded. "Have these bodies dumped over on the west side of the range, Red, and make sure all sign is wiped out. We're rolling now. Nothing can stop us!"

His angry eyes glowed with triumph in the firelight. The great scheme he had evolved, striking at the very heart of Texas — the cattle industry — was working out perfectly. He had no doubt that with the revenge he craved would come a vast fortune.

When he came back to life, Pete Norris felt as though he were being baked in an oven and had long been overdone. The sun was straight overhead, beating down on him with terrible intensity. There was no strength in his limbs. He heard the silver high notes

19

of running water and his mouth was like flannel. For a time, though, he could not crawl toward the liquid sound. Ironically he lay near the rocks he had hoped to reach during the night attack.

His head was a tight drum of dried blood. Besides the scalp crease, so deep that it had missed the brain only by pure luck, there was a groove in his upper arm that stung under the venomous bites of ants and flies.

"Hey, boys!" he called, but only a harsh whisper came from his paralyzed lips.

By terrific will-power Norris managed to move. He was astonished to find his legs would draw up and his arms somehow obey his brain.

Something close at hand flapped up from the rocks, followed by others. The wind of big wings stirred the hot air. Raucous cries, angry and frustrated, came from the hideously bald throats of Mexican vultures. Flies by the million buzzed around, for there was death in the barranca, a feast for all the scavengers of the wilderness.

Pulling himself painfully along, Norris reached the little creek that meandered through the canyon, and began to drink. He bathed his arms and hot face in the wonderful water. But it was some time before he gained enough power to get to his knees.

When he moved, yellow-gray shapes slunk off. The growling coyotes, angered and annoyed by his return to life, were too cowardly to fight for a meal.

At last Pete Norris could stand and take stock of the death scene. He counted the bodies of all his friends. They were dead, every one. Only by some prank of fate had the slug he had taken not killed him. The rustlers had thought him finished and let him lie. The steers and horses were gone. Only a few belongings, blankets and a pair of punctured saddles, had been left. Everything else of value had been taken.

"Blast them!" he muttered. "I'll foller them to the ends of the earth!"

He had suffered physically, but the fact that he had failed the Slash E, his outfit, lost the herd he had collected, drove him on. It made no difference that it wasn't his fault. He was not the breed to search for an excuse.

A familiar whinny made his whirling head perk up. Turning, he looked along the brush-choked ravine and saw his pet mare, Betsy, coming to him with dainty gait. She loved him, so he never hobbled or tied her. In the night, grazing some distance off, she had been missed by the thieves.

They had also left untouched some of the

21

scanty provisions — coffee and flour, dried-beef strips.

"Soon as I get my strength," swore Norris, "I'll hit their trail!"

But it was another thirty-six hours before he could fork a horse without feeling he was going to fall off any minute. The concussion was leaving him, for the shock had been cushioned by the clean living and strength of the youth.

He set out in the first gray of dawn. The trail at first was easy to follow, leading south from the ravine into Brewster County. But there had been a thunder-shower the night before, and the marks of steer hoofs were so thick in the wild rangeland that it was difficult to keep on the right sign. The rustlers, too, had later split up into several bunches, and finding so many divergences confused him.

Mounted on Betsy, he came up on a mesquite-covered ridge and stared out across the broken country. To his left, eastward, he saw the bluish-topped mountain range, blocking any progress in that direction. He shook his head, speaking aloud to the pretty mare.

"No drover in his right mind 'd try to take cows across that range."

Therefore he kept bearing westward. After noon, when he had rested and watered Betsy, he rode on. He struck a cattle trail that wound through the deep grass and chaparral in a southwest line. Buzzards flapped up from his path. The brazen sun was dropping at his right as he reined in the mare, who shied and sniffed in disgust.

Pete Norris dismounted and stepped forward, gun in hand. On the trail lay the body of a man, or what the coyotes and buzzards had left of it. After carefully reconnoitering, for he knew he was on a dangerous trail, Norris examined the corpse. He could see where the bullet had gone through the cheek and into the head. There were other punctures, too. Some iron-gray hair and a mustache told him the dead man had been past middle age. The clothing, too, could be identified.

Suddenly he jumped erect, pushed back into the brush at the side of the path, the gun in his hand at the ready. Sounds had reached his keen ears.

A man came slowly round the bend, riding a range mustang with a Circle 3 on its shoulder. Norris stared at this apparition, which was remarkably thin and hungry-looking, with a large Adam's-apple in its leathery throat, crimson skin, bleached, dry

23

tow hair. It had on cowboy rig, chaps and vest, Stetson, guns.

Norris watched from his bush hiding place. The scrawny waddy took a look at the corpse in the trail but showed little surprise. He swung in his leather and shouted.

"Hey, Miss Sue! C'mere."

Cocking a leg around his horn, he reached in his pocket and drew forth a tobacco plug. He bit a chunk off it and began to chew.

Almost immediately a girl came riding up. She also rode a Circle 3 mount, but her appearance was a great deal more pleasing than the thin man's to Pete Norris. Her beauty was a physical shock to a cow-nurse who had seldom seen women. She was trim and neat in riding clothes and small boots, a light-colored hat over her thick golden hair. Her features were lovely, lips full and red, pearly teeth showing in a gasp of horror as she suddenly caught sight of the thing on the path.

Pete Norris felt his heart contract with deep sympathy at her quick cry. She flung herself from her saddle and bent over the dead man. A scream of agony was torn from her.

"Father! Father!"

Norris stepped out on the path. The

scrawny hombre, still in leather, started in swift suspicion.

"Hey — who're yuh?"

He saw the gun in Norris' hand and stopped reaching toward his Colt handle. Norris was careful to keep his eyes friendly. He had drawn merely to avoid being shot first and questioned later.

"Howdy," he said. "I'm Pete Norris, from the Slash E, Pecos County. Rustlers hit me, wiped out my men and stole a bunch of cows from me. I jest come to and lit out on their trail."

Though watching the man, Norris had really been addressing the young woman. She stood up and stared at his drawn features. She was biting her lips and her eyes were brimming with tears. Norris knew she was fighting for self-control. "How come yuh're so close to Atchinson's body, feller?" demanded the man.

Norris scowled. "Jest come along and seen it. What's yore handle? Where yuh from?"

"My name's Sue Atchinson," the girl replied. "That's my father — dead!"

"He was murdered," Norris told her.

"Yes." Her voice was fairly level. Norris admired her for her control. He could guess the suffering she was undergoing. "This is 'Rooster' Sprague, Mr. Norris. Our ranch foreman."

Rooster Sprague grunted a greeting at the introduction.

"I'll take care of yore dad's body, Miss Sue. Yuh better get on home now."

Sue Atchinson nodded. Pete clicked his tongue and Betsy came strolling up to him.

"Can I ride yore way, ma'am?" he asked.

She mounted, her slim shoulders still bowed. Under the golden tan her face was pale, but she had pride that refused to let her break down.

The Circle 3 ranch lay ten miles southwest, in a grassy valley. Holes and windmills supplied the water necessary to support men and animals. Through the ride, Sue had said little. To divert her mind from the horror of seeing her dead father, Norris told her what had occurred when the rustlers had attacked.

As they pulled into the yard, Norris tried to help her unsaddle. She insisted on doing it herself, and they turned their horses into a corral.

"Come in and have a drink and something to eat," she said absently.

Sue led the way to the kitchen. There were several hands working for the spread, but the girl told him they had been out hunting her father and the four waddies who had mysteriously disappeared. Rooster Sprague had last seen them riding up to the north of the spread. Finally, as Norris had seen, she had found the body of her father.

"I expected he was dead," she said quietly, "when he didn't come in. We've lost so much stock that Dad was furious. He was hunting the thieves. There have been complaints from all over the country. They say it's the worst epidemic of rustling ever known."

"Reckon I oughta know," Norris stated.

"If you'll excuse me, I'll go in and wash up," the girl said.

"Yes, ma'am." Pete Norris watched her trim, girlish figure, the curly hair at the back of her pretty head. "I'd shore like to help her," he muttered. "She's mighty brave."

After he had eaten, he rolled a quirly and strolled outside. It was near nightfall. As he leaned against the house wall, he caught a sound that hurt him terribly, made him want to fight.

It was Sue, crying in her room, her heart broken by the murder of her dad.

"Yeah, I'll get even," vowed Norris, feeling the hot blood flush his cheeks. "Them same rustlers must've run over Atchinson as hit me."

Through the Southwest there were others

— women and children, daughters, wives and sons — mourning their dead. A black pall of horror had struck the cattle industry, the life-stream of Texas.

Chapter III
Texas Lawman

Ranger Jim Hatfield, Captain Bill McDowell's greatest officer and strong right arm in maintaining law in Texas, stepped with panther-like, silent tread into the chief's Austin office. McDowell's shaggy brows were set in a somber expression, his faded blue eyes flashing sparks that meant hell to pay for defiers of the law. He scowled, nodded, gun-gnarled fists tight.

"The cow business, Hatfield," he growled, "is the life-blood of Texas!"

It was said that Bill McDowell could have charged hell with a water-pistol and won out. Now too old for the long, hard trail of fighting owl hooters, Captain Bill had to depend on others. True to form, McDowell picked the mightiest exponent of decency who ever rode the gun-infested, murderous routes of the Southwest. For a thousand miles the huge Lone Star State ranged, bigger than many European countries, without local law in whole sections, wild, feral and on the prod.

Tall as he was, McDowell was topped by the great Ranger. Well over six feet, Jim Hatfield's broad, deep-chested figure tapered to the lean hips of the true fighting man. At the ends of his long arms were thin but strong, wiry hands, well kept and supple. With blinding accuracy they could whip out the two six-guns which hung in oiled, fine black holsters at his waist.

His gray-green eyes, shaded by long black lashes, could darken in anger to the iciness of an Arctic sea. His features were rugged, their grimness softened by a wide mouth above the craggy jaw. He wore leather pants, a blue shirt and vest, a Stetson like any other range rider. His black hair was smoothed back under his wide hat, his skin a golden bronze, his whole being vital with perfect health. Breath-taking coordination of brain, muscle and instinct made the Ranger the terror of law-breakers from the Panhandle to the Rio, from the Gulf to red-hot El Paso.

"No more nerves than a tombstone," thought McDowell, eying his favorite lawman. "Never see the hombre could match him." Aloud the grizzled old fighter ordered: "Sit down, Hatfield. We got to figger this out careful-like. It may mean life or death

29

for Texas."

The grim jaw tightened, the gray-green eyes were grim for a moment as the great officer sat down in the chair opposite Mc-Dowell. The captain cleared his throat and put on a pair of silver-rimmed spectacles which had window glass instead of lenses. They were only for effect and McDowell usually forgot them. The captain rustled a sheaf of official-looking papers.

"As I said, the beef business is Texas' mainstay, Jim. In the last three months there's been a step-up in rustlin' throughout the entire country. I'd say around five hundred per cent more'n usual. Complaints've come in from twenty different counties, from the Oklahoma border to the Rio. Murder goes along with it, when the thieves 're interfered with. Been two dozen reported, prob'ly more we ain't heard tell of."

"No center?" Hatfield asked softly.

His voice was surprisingly gentle for so large a man. That Southern, drawling politeness had fooled more than one gunman into thinking he had an easy proposition on his hands.

"That's the hell of it!" McDowell swore. "I've noted the step-up in rustlin' and I ordered what Rangers been out to keep a

30

sharp look-out. But you savvy what we got to contend with in such a big country. Them brand-blotters're slippery as eels, and once they got a start, yuh never ketch up. But jest this mornin' I got a letter from Sue Atchinson, the first straw I found to grab hold of. Here, look it over."

Hatfield took the letter and read it swiftly.

Dear Uncle Bill:

Dad is dead. His body was found, shot several times, north of the ranch. I'm sure rustlers did it. They've been very lively lately and Dad was frantic. All our best stuff was stolen and he was in debt. He was after them, and so was the Association. I don't know just what I'll do, maybe run the ranch with my foreman's help. A young man named Pete Norris from the Slash E, Pecos County, rode here. He claims he lost a herd to rustlers northeast of our spread. Several of his boys were killed and he was badly wounded. He trailed them down here, but they broke up and covered their sign. I feel awful about Dad —

There was more, ending with love and kisses and signed "Sue."

"I'm her godfather," said McDowell

31

gruffy. "Atchinson always was a live-wire when it come to chasin' stock thieves, even in his young days. He was president of the Brewster County Stock-Raisers, and as such was interested in stoppin' rustlin' over and above pussonal considerations. His Circle Three used to pay well. From what Sue says, though, they've lost their best stock in the past year."

"Reckon a run to this Circle Three district might pay, as a start," Hatfield said. "And that Slash E waddy cinches it."

"Yep. The nearest town to the Circle Three country is Warwick, on the Southern Pacific, south of the Comanche Mountains, Jim. Yuh got to round the mountains to reach it, though. The spur cuts off the section where Atchinson's stand. Yuh'll find Mayor 'Peewee' Cort of Warwick a man to ride the river with. Sheriff Tad Durban's headquarters 're in Warwick. He's head lawman of Brewster County. I dunno anything 'bout him, since he was elected jest last fall. Another thing — the Brewster County Stockmen's Union meets at Warwick on the twelfth, and yuh can learn plenty there."

Hatfield nodded, rose and started for the exit. McDowell watched him quizzically.

"Rustler skunks 're dangerous to come upon sudden-like, Hatfield," the captain warned.

The tall Ranger glanced back over his broad shoulder. For a moment his even, white teeth flashed in a brief smile.

"Reckon to come up with 'em is what he's most anxious to do," McDowell muttered.

Rising, he went to stare out the window at the Ranger, who was throwing a long leg over the saddle of his horse. The magnificent golden sorrel awaiting him sheened with rippling, powerful muscles.

"Him and that Goldy cayuse 're one tough pair," thought the old captain, and nostalgic memories of his own riding days returned to haunt him.

Goldy was in a playful mood. He feigned to buck as his master settled in leather, the rifle sheathed in the saddle holster. After rearing and sunfishing, the handsome golden gelding straightened out to a steady pace, headed west.

Jim Hatfield had come up against cattle thieves before and bested them, but never had he ridden toward so gigantic a criminal outfit as now faced him. As yet he had no idea of the spreading criminal roots of the powerful organization in southwest Texas. Nor had McDowell an inkling of the size of the problem and the terrific dangers against which he had sent his star Ranger. Had the old captain known, he might have hesitated to send even such a man as Hatfield on this dread mission.

Days later, Jim Hatfield rode the dust-caked sorrel across a rolling prairie plateau, interspersed by clumps of scrub trees and high red buttes. A couple of inches in the bottom of one canteen was all that remained of his water supply. He had not eaten for two days, having consumed the last of his provisions in the swift, hard drive for Brewster County. Another night was coming on. Goldy must rest and could not go much longer without water.

"No reason why we shouldn't eat, though," grunted the Ranger. "Plenty of beer 'round."

For miles he had ridden near bunches of range cattle marked with a Star 8. As he came up on a rise, he saw the steel rails of a single-track railroad spur that ran north and south. They were somewhat rusted and the ties were not imbedded. Plainly it was some side-line, perhaps to a large private ranch.

He might have followed the track to its northern hinge and come out somewhere, but he preferred to keep to the west route and hit Warwick as soon as possible. Another twenty-four hours of endurance, he estimated, would see them at the town where

Mayor Peewee Cort lived.

According to range custom, a hungry wanderer had the right to feed himself. The Ranger, unshipping his rifle, rode toward a bunch of steers that were feeding on the grama grass clumps a couple of miles off. They were half-wild and moved off as they saw him coming. But one was slower, a steer with a lame leg. Hatfield threw the Winchester to his shoulder, hardly seeming to take aim. The gun cracked, echoing over the low domes, and the steer dropped in his tracks.

Dismounting, the Ranger took out his long knife, sharpened it on a stone, and knelt by the carcass to cut himself some steaks from the loin. He carved a chunk of hide out of the way, skilfully trained in what he was doing. As he was engrossed in the task of supplying himself with fresh meat, suddenly what sounded like a giant hornet buzzed past his ear and plugged into the dirt beyond, spurting up sand.

He whirled, snatching for the rifle he had laid carefully on the rocks nearby. A second slug skimmed across the flesh of his left forearm, and the blood followed in its wake. Hatfield threw a fresh shell into the firing-chamber, at the same time whirling to face his attackers.

They were up to the north, on the other

side of the track. Half a dozen mounted hombres in Stetsons, they were shooting from standing mustangs.

A third slug missed him, shrieking overhead. The Ranger sent a couple of long ones back, aiming high to shake them. The bullets came close, for the men swung and retreated north, quickly dropping from out of sight.

"Huh," he growled. "A mighty warm welcome we're gettin', Goldy."

The sorrel nuzzled his slim hand as he mounted. He kept his eyes on the bushy rise behind which the cowboys had dropped. As he started away from there, a whole pack of riders, evidently reinforcements, joined the first six. The entire gang came howling over the hill at him.

Hastily the Ranger figured his chances. There were two dozen yelling, spurring waddies cutting down to head him off. The sorrel had been going under the hot sun all day and needed water. A chance would mean at least the danger of a stray bullet hitting Goldy before the swift gelding could pull away.

He spurted toward a big red butte a quarter-mile off. With lead whistling too close for comfort, they made it without any more injury. Leaping from leather, rifle in hand, he left Goldy in the shelter of the rocks. He crouched at the south side of the butte, waiting for his pursuers to come up.

As they approached, firing six-guns and short rifles that chipped shale from the red rocks covering Hatfield, he studied them. They wore cowboy duds and Stetsons, rode range mustangs branded on the flank with a star and some inside figure he couldn't make out. He guessed it was an 8, the same as on the steers.

"Come outa there, damn yuh!" roared a waddy, spurring in foolhardily.

The Ranger's Winchester barked. The hombre's hat strap snapped as the bullet ventilated the crown and cut his hair. The closeness of it frightened the rider to his senses. He whirled off, riding a circle to rejoin his mates. When they stopped at this exhibition of shooting, Hatfield saw his chance.

"Who are yuh?" he called. "I'm a stranger, on my way to Warwick. I jest stopped to pick up a bite of beef, bein' hungry. If yuh come closer though, I'll shoot to kill."

They conferred among themselves, heads together, out of easy range. Another pair of riders appeared. They paused to look down at the steer the Ranger had been butchering when interrupted, then spurred toward the crowd.

One of them seemed to be a chief. He wore a dark suit and black hat, its brim narrower than the usual curving Stetson. He listened to the account his hombres gave, then swung to peer curiously at the point where the Ranger crouched in the rocks. Riding out in front of his boys, he called in a precise, cool voice.

"Hey, you! If you're an honest man, come out. No harm 'll be done you. I'm George Vane of the Star Eight Ranch."

Hatfield rose up, grabbed the sorrel, mounted and rode toward Vane. He kept the boss between himself and the group of waddies, so they could not get a clear bead on him without endangering their chief.

As he came up, he saw that Vane, a good-sized man with slim waist and broad shoulders, had a strong face, sharply chiseled features, with snappy black eyes. His black hair was smooth and glistening under the straight hat. His shirt was clean, and all his gear was natty, well kept and in order. The crisp, close-clipped black mustache was even and topped a thin-lipped, straight mouth that was depressed slightly at the corners. Two vertical wrinkles bit deep at the top of his sharp nose.

"Howdy, Vane," drawled the Ranger. "My name's Jim Harris, I'm a cowhand, come from the Panhandle, ridin' west to Warwick. Stopped to get some steak, didn't figger the country wasn't hospitable. Up where I come from it's okay for a stranger to carve himself a meal, long as he does it open-like and chooses a steer that ain't much account. Well, I did likewise."

The dark, hard eyes drilled him. Evidently the open, honest expression of the rugged waddy convinced Vane. "Okay, stranger. I saw the cow you killed. It's plain you're no rustler. That's what upset my boys, they saw you bendin' over a cow and jumped to the conclusion you were a brand-blotter. Been a lot of it lately in these parts. If you're hungry, ride up to the ranch and eat."

"How far is it?"

"Oh, an hour's ride north, that's all. Come on." Vane swung in saddle, scowling at the silent man. "You boys be careful with your lead. If you'd taken a good look at that cow, you'd have seen that this waddy was carving himself a steak, not running a brand."

CHAPTER IV
WRECKING A SALE

Jim Hatfield rode alongside George Vane north to the shallow, great valley in which stood a ranchhouse, barns, corrals — a tremendous, going concern. The wood of the buildings was fairly new, not yet weathered black by the sun. This was where the railroad spur stopped, a private line to the Southern Pacific, as he had figured. Food, water and a bed were given the rider. The bunkhouse eventually filled with riders for the large outfit. Everything seemed to be in perfect order to the Ranger. He was worn out and glad to sleep.

In the morning, he woke to the familiar sounds of a ranch at work, the calls of cowboys, the thud of mustang hoofs. The smell of coffee and frying beef and potatoes was in the keen air, not yet heated by the rising sun.

Hatfield ate a hearty meal and went to call Goldy, who had rested in pasture through the night. He saddled up, then rolled himself a quirly and started toward the ranchhouse to thank George Vane for his hospitality before riding on for Warwick.

Far to the west rose the high Comanches, blocking the direct route that way for mile on mile, tapering off to the south. Toward the north the end of the hills was invisible from the Star 8. They made a fine barrier, for no steer would ever cross their jagged ridges. A tall hombre smoking on the veranda step looked up, nodded to him as he rounded the porch.

"Vane's gone. Rode out early for town. Won't be back till day after tomorrer."

Hatfield left his thanks by proxy. Astride the sorrel, he swung southwest for Warwick.

The town sprawled along the S.P. tracks, roasted by a golden, soul-searing sun that dried out every ounce of moisture from man, beast, the sandy earth and the planks of the frame houses.

As Jim Hatfield rode along the rutted main street, which paralleled the gleaming, red-hot steel lines, the dust puffed up from under Goldy's hoofs. The Ranger quickly memorized the settlement, built along both sides of the iron road.

The frame buildings faced one another across the wide space down which the tracks ran. The majority were one story high, but a few were more pretentious. The Drovers Hotel was a three-story place, bulking huge among its smaller neighbors. There were two large saloons and dancehalls, a rambling general store, a couple of chow places, a jail

41

and sheriff's office with a barred window.

All Southwest towns had a plaza. Warwick was no exception, the scrofulous, beaten ground between the two lines of buildings forming the commons here. South of the tracks, and running eastward for a mile, were strong cattle-pens. Side paths ran north and south, petering out after a few small unpainted shacks gave up and the bushy prairie took command.

Save for scrubs, there were no trees nearby. The water-tower tank on the railroad formed a landmark for miles. To the north reared the brown summits of the Comanche Mountains, heavily timbered.

"Plenty of folks in town," muttered the tall Ranger.

His throat was dry as old leather. The trip from Austin had been made in swift time and it had thinned man and horse down. They were coated with grayish dust from the day's run, though the stop at the Star 8 had been a help.

The hitch-racks outside the awnings above the wooden walks were crowded with saddle horses and wagons that afternoon. A few people walked sluggishly here and there, but mostly they were seeking shade from the strong Texas sun.

Pausing outside the Drovers Hotel at the

watering trough, the Ranger let the sorrel drink. Then he rode to the livery stable, where he saw to it that Goldy was rubbed down, fed and turned out into a corral.

Hatfield, stiff from days in leather, rolled over to the Drovers Hotel for a good wash. Spruced up, a fresh bandanna at his bronzed throat, the tall officer strode along the wooden walk.

Ben Walton's Chow House

The sign attracted him. He was hungry for town food, so he swung through the open door.

"Town's crowded, ain't it, ma'am?" he asked in his soft drawl of the pretty waitress who brought ham and eggs and coffee.

She was young and her eyes had already softened at sight of the tall, rugged stranger in the prime of manhood.

"Yes, sir," she replied, surprised at her own docility. Usually her tongue was sharp and quick with the waddies who came in. "There's a meeting of the Stockmen's Association. Lots of folks brought their women along."

"Thanks." The long-lashed, gray-green eyes caught the feminine blue ones for a moment. "Is Mayor Cort around?"

43

"You'll find him at the New York Saloon if he isn't at home," said the waitress. She glanced out the window. "There he goes now, into the New York with Sheriff Durban and Mister Walton. Ben Walton runs this place. He's my boss. The mayor's that little man with the white hair and the scar on his cheek."

Finishing his meal, Hatfield paid, nodded a grave good-by to the palpitating waitress, and went out. The sun was low in the sky. A hot breeze was coming up from the southwest. Heat haze lay over the land.

The New York was crowded with ranchers, waddies and townsmen, shuffling around in the sawdust that padded the floor. From the dancehall at the side came the music of a piano and violin, the scrape of boots at the unfamiliar art of dancing.

Mayor Cort was easy to pick out. The little fellow had on corduroy pants tucked into neat half-boots, a dark shirt and string tie, Stetson big enough to overshadow his vibrant, small body. His white hair, eyebrows and neat mustache were touched by the rime of age, with a scarred, round face and straight blue eyes. Peewee Cort spoke in a shrill voice that was loud for the whole saloon to hear.

"I tell yuh what we need is vigilantes,

Sheriff! The rustling's worse'n it ever was. The short end of a rope's the only way."

Cort shook his glass of whiskey under Tad Durban's long nose, which twitched over his ragged black mustache. The Ranger took in the sheriff, whose five-pointed star was pinned to the blue vest over the stout, wide chest. Durban was swarthy of skin, eyes black and close. He was heavily loutish, would tip the scales at over 250. Durban removed his furred black Stetson to mop his bald spot with a red bandanna.

"I'm the law in Brewster, Cort," he growled. "And I'll come up with 'em. Won't we, Ben?"

At the sheriff's other fat flank stood a large man with light hair, wide mouth, and blue eyes. They all seemed to crease in a grin as his superior addressed him for confirmation.

"Dawggone, Sheriff, you know me. I'm with yuh. But at that there's somethin' in what the mayor says. These cattle thieves're plumb lively and they're gettin' worse by the minute."

Durban shrugged his hulking shoulders, drained off his glass. Wiping his ragged mustache with the back of a hair-flecked hand as big as a pig's hind leg, he swung around on tremendous feet.

"I got to see to the meetin' hall, Peewee. C'mon, Walton."

Trailed by his tall, blue-eyed deputy, who turned and winked back at Cort, Durban left the New York. The Ranger edged up the bar till he was close to Mayor Cort's ear.

"Cort," he said, voice so low that only Peewee heard, "MacDowell sent me over on the rustlin' business. I'm Ranger Jim Hatfield."

Cort turned startled eyes up to the big man. He licked his thin lips.

"Howdy," he whispered, "What can I do for yuh, Ranger?"

"Like to talk to yuh, quiet-like. I'll stay undercover till I see what's up."

"Foller me, then."

Ten minutes later the Ranger sat in Cort's kitchen.

"Yeah, the rustlin's terrible," reported Cort. "A lotta killin', too, and the thieves 're smart and very powerful. We can't seem to come up with 'em."

"I savvy. Sounds like they're really organized. McDowell heard from a young lady, Sue Atchinson of the Circle Three. I wanta talk to her. How far's her spread?"

"Yuh're in luck. Sue's in town today and yuh won't hafta ride to hell-and-gone to the Circle Three. It's way up north, behind the

46

Comanche mountains. She's a mighty sweet gal, is Sue. Mebbe yuh savvy her dad was president of the Brewster County stockmen. They'll elect a new boss tonight, Atchinson bein' dead."

"So Sue's in Warwick," mused Hatfield. "Where can I find her?"

"Well, at five o'clock —" Cort took out a gold turnip watch attached to a thick chain with a bull's-head fob — "she'll be sellin' her ranch to the Syndicate. It's most five now. Soon as she's through yuh can talk to her."

"Yeah? What's she sellin' for?"

Cort shrugged. "Oh, the Circle Three stock was pretty well cleaned-out by rustlers, Hatfield. Anyhow a woman can't run a big spread very well."

The tall Ranger stood up.

"S'pose yuh take me over now and introduce me as yore nephew. Call me Jim Harris."

Five minutes later Hatfield stood in a square room attached to the general store. Around the table sat several people, among them Sue Atchinson. The Ranger also saw George Vane of the Star 8, the good-looking hombre he had met the day before on the range.

Hatfield's grave eyes took in the gathering. Vane was sitting next to the young woman. She was pretty as a picture with her thick golden hair uncovered, her full red lips half-parted as she read over some legal papers. But there was a sad look in her youthful blue eyes. On the other side sat a thin, scrawny hombre with a prominent Adam's apple and leathery, florid skin. He had removed his Stetson, revealing bleached, dried-out tow hair.

"I hate to sell," breathed Sue. "It doesn't seem right."

"It's the only thing to do, ma'am," the scrawny fellow said quickly. "We can't make a go of it."

Hatfield stepped forward. Peewee Cort touched Miss Atchinson's soft arm.

"Sue, I'd like yuh to meet up with my nephew, Jim Harris. He's come down to these parts to visit me."

The young woman looked up into the long-lashed, gray-green eyes. She smiled fleetingly.

"Glad to know you, Jim. This is a sad day for me. I'm selling the Circle Three. Meet my foreman, Rooster Sprague."

"Just sign at the bottom of the pages, Miss Atchinson," urged Vane, annoyed at the interruption. "We'll take possession next week. That'll give you time to pack up."

Hatfield took a chair and squeezed in between the young woman and Rooster Sprague, who reddened with anger.

"I wanted to talk to yuh, ma'am," the Ranger began glibly, ignoring the foreman's scowl. "Why are yuh sellin' out? Uncle says yore spread always paid, up to the last year or two, when the rustlers hit yuh so hard."

"The thieves have taken all our salable stock," she explained. "It would take a couple of years before we could ship again."

"And we can't hold out that long, ma'am," Sprague added impatiently. "This galoot's only wastin' our time."

He sought to shove Hatfield back, but found the tall man too firmly planted to move.

"I was fetched up on a ranch, ma'am, and savvy the angles, rustlin' and all," Hatfield declared blandly. "Why not give it another fling? I'll guarantee yuh won't lose out in the end."

Something like hope sprang into her blue eyes.

"You mean it?" she cried.

"I'm in a hurry, and the meeting's due to start at eight, Miss Atchinson," George Vane broke in. "I have some things to do first. If you wish to sell, let's get it over with. As a matter of fact, my Syndicate won't be able to make much use of your range before several years. However, we're willing to take it off your hands."

"At a song, I'll bet," Hatfield said pleasantly. "Just give me a chance to have a look-see round yore spread, ma'am, and I'll tell yuh whether to sell or not."

Rooster Sprague sprang to his feet with an exclamation of fury.

"Are you sayin' I don't know my business?" he shouted. "I been on the range since I was twelve."

"Quiet," Hatfield stated. "I'm tryin' to talk to this lady."

He was purposely prodding the Circle Three foreman, for Rooster Sprague seemed overeager for Miss Atchinson to sign away her legacy. Rooster Sprague turned several shades redder, lost his head. He slapped Hatfield in the face.

"Yuh danged nosy coyote, I'll take yore hide off if yuh don't get outa here!"

Fear flashed into his red-rimmed eyes as he jumped back. The Ranger was slowly, ominously rising from his seat and turning on him.

"Stand back or I'll drill yuh!" Sprague howled, jumping back to the wall.

Chapter V
Saloon Brawl

Rooster Sprague sought to draw and made it partially, six-gun muzzle clearing its sheath. But Hatfield's long arm flashed out. He gripped the bony wrist. The bullet from the Colt plugged into the floor, kicking up splinters.

Sprague gave a screech of pain. His pistol left his unnerved hand as the Ranger jerked his arm up behind his neck. The gun clanked on the floor. Hatfield kicked it into a corner. Picking up the scrawny foreman, he held him aloft for an instant.

The door was all the way across the room, but there was a window handy. The tall Ranger hurled Sprague through the glass, which crashed as the screaming foreman disappeared from sight.

"There," Jim Hatfield drawled, resuming his seat. "Now we can talk in peace, ma'am."

The whole play had taken but a few seconds. Those in the room had watched with dropped chins as Hatfield disposed of the annoying foreman of the Circle Three. George Vane got up.

"What's your decision, Miss Atchinson?" he asked coldly. "I'm a busy man."

"She's goin' to hold on to the Circle

Three, Vane," Hatfield answered for her. "And I'm runnin' it!"

Sue Atchinson's eyes sparkled as she looked up into the cool, gray-green eyes of the rugged Ranger.

"That's right, Mr. Vane," she cried. "Jim's my new foreman and I won't sell the Circle Three. Sorry I've wasted your time."

George Vane shrugged, and his crisp-mustached lip twitched in a mirthless smile.

"Very well, Miss Sue. A lady has the right to change her mind."

He nodded to Hatfield and left the room, trailed by the lawyer who had made out the necessary deeds for transfer.

"Now, Jim," began Miss Atchinson, "that was mighty brave talk we made. But what do you intend to do? I told you I'm almost cleaned out of salable stock and have no reserve funds to go on."

"I'll have a look-see tomorrer," he promised her. "I got right sharp eyes, ma'am, and mebbe we can find a few head of cattle hidin' out in the draws. Tonight I reckon I'll go to the stockmen's meetin', as yore foreman."

"Good. I'll see you there, then." She smiled up at him and, nodding good-by to Peewee Cort, left the place.

"Well, yuh shore handled Rooster Sprague

quick and efficient, Ranger," the little mayor exclaimed when they were alone. "But what yuh hopin' to gain by takin' charge of the Circle Three?"

"Got to take a hold somewheres," the Ranger replied. "And if rustlers 've hit the Circle Three once, they'll hit her ag'in. As foreman of the Circle Three, I'll be able to circulate as I want in these parts."

"Business always makes my throat dry," Cort said. "S'pose we drift over and have us a drink."

Outside, the sun was a huge ruby ball on the horizon. Night was close at hand. The cowtown was noisy with visitors, ranchers and retainers from far and near, a colorful pageantry of fancy duds and expensive trappings.

The tall Ranger, the peppery little mayor hardly reaching his shoulder, paused on the porch a moment. His level eyes probed nearby corners for Rooster Sprague, who might be seeking vengeance. But the lanky foreman had picked himself up and evaporated.

Mayor Cort led the way to the New York Saloon. They sat down at a table in back and ordered drinks. Indulging in range gossip had always been keenly interesting to Jim Hatfield. As the night dropped its sudden velvet blanket over Warwick, oil lamps, hanging from ceiling rafters, were let down and lighted, then pulled back into place on their ropes. The talk of many men and the strains of music filled the large place.

"Hey, here comes Rooster!" Cort whispered anxiously.

Hatfield had been hunting a wedge so he could squeeze in and contact the cattle thieves striking wholesale through mighty Texas. Now he thought he had it. He watched the scrawny, florid ex-foreman of the Circle 3 as Rooster came hesitantly toward him, both hands in plain sight so there wouldn't be any misunderstanding.

Close to the Ranger's table, Sprague sniffled and shifted his long feet.

"Mister," he began, face redder than ever, "I want to tell yuh I'm mighty sorry 'bout the trouble we had. I'd like to help yuh out there, and Miss Sue, too. If you'll let me, I'll be glad to ride for yuh and wait for my pay."

Rooster blinked as Hatfield caught his washed-out eyes. The strength of the tall waddy had appalled him. Evidently he was playing with dynamite against his will.

"Now what's the idea behind this?" mused the Ranger inwardly. He did not know. He said aloud: "Why, that's mighty fine of yuh,

Rooster. S'pose yuh report at the ranch to-morrer, then I can use yore help, not sav-vyin' the local ropes."

"Then bygones is bygones?"

"Shore. Sit down and have a drink."

"Thanks. I would, but I gotta be ridin', Jim. See yuh tomorrer."

Rooster stuck out a bony hand, gingerly shook with the Ranger. Glad to be going, he swung and left the saloon.

"Huh, yuh converted him pronto," observed Mayor Cort dryly. "Seems to me yuh're as forgivin' as him, son."

Hatfield slowly closed one eye in a wink. Customers were seeping in and out of the saloon, for it was the center of Warwick's entertainment. The stockmen's meeting would take place at eight P. M., in a big warehouse rented for the purpose on the other side of the tracks.

A bartender in a white apron came shouldering through from the front.

"Sheriff wants to speak to yuh, Peewee. He's up the road a piece."

"Okay. I'll be right back, Jim."

The little mayor jumped up and hustled off. Suddenly Hatfield grew aware that a bunch of men, who had recently entered and had just thrown down a round of drinks, had swung from the bar toward him.

Ever alert, he scrutinized them as they slowed close to his table.

Most of them wore cowboy gear, leather pants, Stetson and open vest, bandanna, high-heeled, spurred boots. Some needed a shave, but that was nothing unusual on the range, nor was a hard-eyed, nail-biting expression anything to fight about. Red liquor always inflamed the sons of the plains and they lived a rough, tough life. Hatfield, a genius at noting details, saw that they wore individual get-ups — hats of different hue, nothing uniform about them.

"Doggone," he thought, quick eyes taking in two small, triangular cuts at the left side of each of the dozen Stetsons, "they're ear-marked!"

Every man had this little mark, even the lithe, thin silent Mexican in the van. The dark-skinned Mex wore a high sombrero trimmed with rows of pearl buttons, velvet, tight-fitting bell pants, a red sash. Under the pencil-smear black mustache the brownish lips were thin and cruel.

The Ranger was warned by his sixth sense that told of peril, acquired by long experience in such situations. The dozen waddies backing the Mexican formed a semi-circle, standing so that they hid the seated officer from the main saloon. Nobody was looking at the rear corner, anyway. They were all busy with their own pleasures.

Three feet from Hatfield, the Mex had taken a stand to his left, so he was forced to turn his head to face him.

"Senor," he began, voice low but dripping furious hatred, "I hear what you say! Ees eensult, peeg! Fight eef you dare!"

Francisco de Lira kept his voice down. Only Hatfield and the close-ringing gunnies heard the challenge. Hatfield read death in the shoe-button-black, glowing eyes, which mirrored the hate-filled heart of the Mexican. It was a personal dislike, for de Lira wasn't drunk.

"Better check-rein yoreself, Mex," the Ranger drawled. "I ain't huntin' trouble, but I can take it if it comes."

De Lira, he calculated, was trying to make him start for his gun. He watched the bony brown hands. Only instant-fractions ticked off this quick play. It was all done in a rising rush of murderous attack.

Hatfield figured the Mex to be a knife-man. Such fellows favored that weapon at close range. He caught the flicker of de Lira's left hand, rising to the protruding butt of the six-gun at his snake hip. But at the same moment, the Ranger saw the ripple of muscles in the Mexican's right paw, the panther movement as de Lira bent.

That flaunting of the left hand was but a feint to engage the Ranger's eye while de Lira put into play the long, razor-sharp fang concealed in a leg sheath. The Mexican crouched, ready to rip up through Hatfield's vitals to the heart as he straightened his legs.

De Lira's speed and skill were phenomenal. He got his knife into action as swiftly as any first-class gunfighter could pull a six-shooter. While his body was low, his head weaving like a rattler poised to strike, he had the advantage over the seated Ranger.

There was no time to rise, to tilt the chair away from the snaky brown hand. With all de Lira's weight behind it, the hand tautened about the stag handle. The twelve-inch steel blade abruptly was a scintillating blur of death in the saloon lamplight. Fast as Jim Hatfield was in action, he was seated. With guns bunched at his hips, he couldn't get his Colts going before de Lira hit.

"Ugh!" de Lira's hot breath grunted from his lungs in the exertion of the terrible drive.

He struck with shocking force, but he was the one who yelped in agony. Hatfield had been caught at a disadvantage, but he had fought knifers before. He had known the point at which de Lira would aim. Moreover, his superb coordination of brain and muscle allowed him to turn to his advantage even the fact that he was seated.

His left arm flew up, interposing between the ribs above his heart and the flicking brown hand. There was a sharp crack as de Lira's bony knuckles struck the Ranger's hard forearm. The knife was checked in its drive toward his vitals, only an inch from his ribs.

"*Caramba!*" howled the Mexican.

He drew back like a feinting boxer. The disengaging knife slid across the flesh of the Ranger's arm, cutting through his sleeve and slicing his skin. Blood followed in its wake, gushing from the wound.

But even as he made his unerring move to check the first blow, the Ranger's other hand streaked for his Colt. Shooting from such a position was more difficult than when in a crouch, but he had the weapon out, cocked it with his long, fast thumb.

Black eyes flashing death, de Lira flicked his wrist back to throw, choosing now to use the knife as a missile. The Ranger fired across his knees, the black six-shooter muzzle canted upward.

De Lira took the Ranger lead between his shining, shoe-button eyes. A bluish hole suddenly formed at the top of his sharp eagle-beak. He stood frozen in the last position his muscles had taken in following his punctured brain's mandate.

The explosion of the Ranger's gun electrified the saloon. The echoes drowned to silence the hubbub of voices and music. When the knife dropped in the sawdust, and de Lira fell forward on his face, both sounds were the only audible ones.

"Hold it, gents —" began Jim Hatfield.

The gray-green eyes were dark as an Arctic sea. The wide mouth had the grimness of death. His rugged face was set in menacing lines as he acted with smooth, flowing rhythm, without the slightest hesitation about what he meant to do.

There were a dozen men in that semicircle, de Lira's backers, who had come to cover him while he disposed of the Ranger. They hadn't expected to see anything like this, weren't ready for the sudden reversal. The greatest shock of their lives had been the killing of their leader.

"Drop that skunk!" snarled a squat hombre in boiling fury.

Open-mouthed, the other gunnies watched the last spasmodic movements of the Mexican in the sawdust. Attracted by the shot, the customers were turning to the rear corner, but the standing hombres still hid what had occurred. No man save the attackers could observe the swift moves the Ranger made to even the great odds against himself.

Chapter VI
Plan of Action

Colt still in hand, a grayish plume of smoke oozing from its black muzzle, Hatfield fired under the table top at the squat gunny who had been first to come to his senses and go for his gun after de Lira fell. The killer's six-shooter swiftly cleared leather, barrel rising to murder point as Hatfield snapped a shot his way.

The squat gunny suddenly yiped like a kicked dog as the Ranger lead hit him in the side and spun him around like a gyrating top. His revolver went off, but the dropping muzzle sent the bullet driving into the floor.

The Ranger sprang off his chair, tipping the thick oaken table before him as a shield. The rest of them were drawing, to send a volley into him, riddle him with lead. Two let go. He felt his Stetson jump and strain against the chin strap as a slug ventilated the high crown. Another whistled past his ear and smacked into the wall, flipping out splinters.

He fired with one gun, drawing his second. Behind the protection of the table top, he fanned bullets into the closely packed killers who sought his life.

The shouts of excited men rose to pandemonium in the New York Saloon. Most of the innocent bystanders, not wishing to be involved in a gunfight of which they knew nothing, ducked for cover. They took to the shelter of the bar or ran into the other rooms. The acrid powder-smoke drifted up as heavy Colts barked in a duel of hate between the attackers and Jim Hatfield.

The sickening thud of lead in flesh and bone, the deafening reverberations of the booming pistols, the gasped curses of fighting men, were almost a single sound in the swift affray.

"Get him, blast yuh, get him!" shouted a gunny lieutenant.

He died with an oath on his twisted lips, Ranger lead finding his heart. Thick and fast the Ranger bullets, directed by a cool brain and the strong heart which never speeded its beat to spoil muscular action, sprayed the churning mob of killers.

The main fight lasted but half a minute. Yet in that time Hatfield had emptied both guns, and the others had sent more than fifty slugs his way. Some had struck the table top, deflecting as they came through, taking big splinters with them. But most had gone high or low, the aim of the gunmen shaken by the blaring hot breath of the Ranger Colts.

Suddenly they broke. Singing death about their ears, the survivors out there realized that half their number had gone down. The agonized screams of a wounded gunny was what finally cracked their nerve.

Hatfield dropped his hot weapons and grabbed at the fancy Colts in de Lira's holsters, a couple of feet from him as he crouched behind the table. He got one, cocked it, ready for further action, but that was unnecessary.

The six ran, panic striking their hearts. They turned and split up, diving for windows and doors, any way to escape the deadly lead of the super-fighter they had come to kill. A couple of shots hurried them on their way. Glass crashed, for one could not stop to open the window.

Quiet fell over the big room. It was a quiet as stunning as the noise which had preceded it. Ear-drums still banged with the explosions of the big .45s. Smoke and light sawdust particles filled the shafts from the lamps like motes in a sunbeam.

Abruptly the startling silence was broken

by the cursing screech of the wounded gunny. He began to laugh like a hyena as he went delirious.

Jim Hatfield cleared his throat, coughed, straightened up from behind his table. He picked up his six-guns, coolly reloaded them and let them slide into their supple, pleated black holsters.

His left arm was still bleeding. There were two holes in his Stetson, giving good ventilation, and half a dozen rips in his clothing. Across his cheek was a thin brown line, a singe from another slug. One of his half-boots had had a chunk shot from the high heel.

Hatfield's ears were still ringing, and the terrific fight had brought the sweat of concentration to his forehead and bronzed cheeks. The knife slash in his arm itched and burned, dripped blood to the floor as he stood there, booted feet wide, watching to see if any more foes came at him.

"Hey, you!" a bartender hailed him from behind the long counter. "What's the idea, shootin' us up?"

"No particular idea," drawled the tall Ranger. "I don't shoot unless somebody fires first."

Voices began rising throughout the saloon. The Ranger was a stranger in town, so suspicious looks were cast his way.

A couple of the men on the sawdust floor needed attention, and Hatfield wanted to bandage up his own arm. He slid toward an open side door, stepped out into the darkness, moving with supple speed.

Heading toward the main street, he heard the long-drawn whistle of an approaching train. The rumble of steel on steel drew closer, and an express flashed by. Roaring through the little cowtown, the earth-shaking vibration dominated all other sounds before it receeded.

Jim Hatfield, pausing at the corner, of the saloon, saw Mayor Peewee Cort come galloping up and start into the New York Bar.

"Cort!" he hailed softly.

The mayor swung toward him, sighed with relief.

"I heard gunshots, figgered somethin' was wrong," he growled.

"There was. Bunch of hombres I never saw before tried to pick a fight with me."

It had all been too deliberate for the Mexican knifeman and his mates to have happened along by accident. Peewee Cort had been removed from the table at the moment of attack, and there was Rooster Sprague's visit —

"Sprague shook hands with me, pointed

me out for 'em," mused Hatfield. Then he asked aloud: "What'd Sheriff Durban want of yuh, Peewee?"

"Oh, Durban didn't want nothin' important," Cort answered. "Jest askin' 'bout what he oughta say at the meetin'."

More than ever, Hatfield was suspicious. He was well aware that Peewee Cort had been called out so there would be no witness on his side after the shooting. His brooding eyes searched the plaza and the busy streets. The warehouse in which the meeting was to take place was brightly lit, its doors open. A few early comers were sauntering in, and groups of sturdy Texas cowmen stood out front, smoking and chatting as they waited for the meeting to begin.

"I can't stand here," the Ranger drawled, keeping his ideas to himself as was his wont. "Let's drift over to yore place so I can spruce up and bandage this here wound. Then we'll head for the meetin'."

"Right. C'mon, that arm's got a nasty slash in it."

"They picked me quick," thought the Ranger. "I nosed in on that deal, prevented Sue Atchinson from turnin' her Circle Three over to Vane's Syndicate. Next thing, that fancy Mex knifeman tries to hang my hide on the wall as a souvenir. But are they the rustlers I'm after?"

He needed another connection to hook up the attack on himself with the range thieves who had struck for hundreds of miles across Texas.

At eight o'clock Jim Hatfield, towering at the side of the tiny Mayor Cort, strode into the meeting of the Brewster County Stockmen. Wall lamps were lighted. Up at one end was a rough board platform so the speakers could stand higher than the heads of the audience. Planks had been nailed on boxes to form benches, and these were already crowded with ranchers.

Many of these people had come from miles away to the meeting. The Brewster organization, an affiliate of the Southwest Drovers, was an important branch of the Texas stock-raising industry. There were representatives here from other counties, who had come by rail or taken a week to ride to Warwick.

The Ranger quietly sat down beside the mayor at the end of a long plank bench, and took in the honest folks about him. They were, he knew, the heart and soul of mighty Texas. Hard-working and brave, they raised the beef on which the Nation fed. Upon them depended the welfare of the State itself. They had made Texas great, and their misfortune was a prime concern of the Rangers.

There were women present, wives and daughters who had come with their men. Not far away sat pretty Sue Atchinson. She caught Hatfield's eye and smiled at him.

George Vane arrived with a half dozen big young fellows in cowboy duds, guns on, and took seats across the hall. On the platform were several Texans, stalwart ranchers, men of responsibility, the officers of the union.

"Who's that?" Hatfield asked Cort, indicating a burly, red-faced hombre who seemed to be an authority.

"Huh? Oh, that's Brant Tazewell, now head of the Association. He was vice-president, but Pop Atchinson bein' dead, Tazewell'll take charge. That thin feller with the white hair and scar on his cheek is Cimarron Jones, the secretary. The fat one's John Olliphant, treasurer. All of 'em own brands in Brewster. See that hombre in the black suit? That's Drew Perry, from the Panhandle. He's a big shot up there."

Cort pointed out and named the various important Texas stock-raisers. Then Brant Tazewell stood before the audience, raising his arms for quiet. They quickly fell into silence.

"Folks," he began, "we're meetin' tonight

for important matters. There's to be an election to choose a new president. Yuh all savvy what happened to Pop Atchinson, our beloved leader. He was shot down on his own range."

A wave of anger growled over the gathering.

"First in every man's mind is this rustlin' that's hit us so hard," Tazewell went on. "I got figgers on recent stock losses and they're sky-high. Nothin' like it was ever seen before in Texas. Sixty thousand head of first-class steers took from Brewster ranches alone, to say nothin' of eighteen range riders killed in performance of their duty, tryin' to check the thieves."

His broad, honest face grew red as a beet as he slammed a fist into his hand.

"My best stock's been stole, and I savvy plenty of yuh are in the same pickle. We ain't been able to come up with the rustlers, leastways not in large enough force to take 'em. They're thick as autumn leaves!"

Jim Hatfield listened carefully. After Tazewell had summed up, others spoke. Men from the audience rose and reported recent outrages of the ruthless gangs stripping the Texas range of beef. They all demanded action. Some shouted to form a vigilante band to hunt down the criminals, others cried that the Rangers be called in.

For an hour they yelled back and forth. The only thing agreed on was that the rustling must be stopped or they would all go bankrupt. Then they paused to elect Tazewell president in the dead Atchinson's place, and they chose another vice-president.

In the lull, the tall waddy rose and asked for the floor.

"Who are yuh, mister?" Tazewell asked. "I don't recognize yuh."

"My name's Jim Harris," Hatfield replied.

"He's my nephew, Brant," called Peewee Cort.

"And he's my new foreman," Sue Atchinson told them. "He's in charge of the Circle Three from now on."

Hatfield faced the big meeting. Though he was a stranger to them, they felt the big fellow's strength and power. The magnificent specimen of Texas manhood standing before them could not fail to impress them. Eagerly they listened to his soft but effective voice.

"Folks, I've had experience with stock thieves. 'Course this is the biggest yet, but they all work the same, large or small. First they pick a lonely range and drive off what they want. They go fast and make shore they ain't trailed. Once away, they use a runnin' iron to change the brand, and finally they got to market the stolen beef. This gang, or bunch of gangs, must have a big depot somewheres to sell the stuff they've took. What we need to do most is find this center.

"To do so, we got to come up with some of the thieves and trail 'em by sight. Here's the way to do it, I figger. Yuh can pick range patrols — men who ride the line huntin' rustlers. At a few points we'll have bands of fightin' men ready to ride out at an instant's notice. The range rider spottin' any rustlers, instead of tryin' to stop 'em, must foller at a distance till he can send word back to us. Onct we spot their depots, we'll be able to hit 'em in full force."

A murmur of satisfaction went through the big meeting and the eyes that fixed the tall Ranger were admiring. He had given them an excellent, workable plan.

There was a quick stir at a side door behind Hatfield, who was watching the eager faces of the cowmen he was addressing.

"Hey, what's all this?" demanded Brant Tazewell.

"Throw up yore paws, damn yuh," growled a thick voice behind the Ranger, "or I'll blow yuh inside out!"

71

He felt the hard steel of a double-barreled shotgun rammed into his back ribs.

Chapter VII
Arrest

Jim Hatfield didn't wish to start a shooting affray in the crowded room, with women about. Besides, with the cocked, sawed-off shotgun against him, he could have only a Chinaman's chance of escaping sudden death. The audience had been engrossed in his earnest words and several men had quietly slipped inside, behind the officer and Mayor Peewee Cort. Slowly the slim hands went up. From the corner of his eye, the Ranger looked to see who had him covered.

It was Sheriff Durban scowling at him, shotgun gripped in pudgy hands, fingers through the trigger-guard. The five-pointed badge glinted on his blue vest. Plainly the loutish, swarthy sheriff was furious at the big fellow he held under his gun.

"What's wrong, Tad?" demanded Cort sharply.

"This feller shot and killed a Mexican at the New York Saloon this evenin'," replied Durban hotly. "When the corpse's friends tried to horn in and stop it, Harris plugged several of 'em, without any provocation. It's still a crime to kill a man in this town, ain't it?"

"Jim wouldn't do such a thing," declared Cort. "He was set upon."

"How do you know what happened?" Durban argued sullenly. "You was talkin' to me when the scrap begun."

There were deputies with the sheriff to make the arrest — a saloon bartender from the New York, Walton, the chow-place owner, as well as three of the gunnies who had sought to finish Hatfield off in the brawl.

"That's the hombre who downed poor Francisco," cried one of the killers shrilly, pointing accusingly at Hatfield. "He yanked a six-shooter and let go without warnin'. Then he gunned us, downed three and there ain't one of us got a whole hide. It was cold murder!"

Legally, Hatfield realized, they had him. The sheriff had no choice but to arrest on such a story, and they would swear away his life. He was not eager to disclose his identity as a Texas Ranger. His hidden enemies were after him, seeking to get him out of the way. If they discovered who he was, they might grow alarmed and draw off, spoil his chance of catching up with them. He was not yet ready to show his hand, nor did he desire to

73

buck the local law — if the local law, represented by Durban, were honest.

"Say, who was this Mex yuh say he killed?" demanded Peewee Cort, seeking a loophole to extricate Hatfield.

Hatfield caught Cort's eye, shook his head and frowned, so the mayor wouldn't blurt that he was a Ranger.

"Francisco de Lira was a poor, honest, hard-workin' Mexican," one of the lying witnesses insisted. "I knowed him for years. He was a line rider for Don Carlos, across the Rio in Chihuahua. He never hurt no-body in his life."

Menacing guns bristled around the tall waddy. George Vane, boss of the Star 8, an influential rancher, jumped up, his face red.

"I know that big man!" he declared. "He's mighty fast with his guns and anxious to use 'em, folks. Yesterday some of my boys caught him bending over a steer on my spread, but he explained it away and I believed him. And this afternoon I saw him throw Rooster Sprague, of the Circle Three, through a window. He seems to get out of one scrape and into another."

Sheriff Durban reached in a hip pocket, keeping his shotgun up with one hand. He held out an iron bar with a rounded hook on one end.

"It's ag'in the county law," he said, "to tote one of these. Found it in his gear, hid inside his poncho."

The piece of metal was a running iron, illegal in Texas. Brands could too easily be run over with such irons.

"A hunderd to one," shouted a waddy near Vane, "he's a rustler and spy, gents! Let's settle his hash here and now."

"They're shore after me," mused the Ranger, "plantin' that runnin' iron and all."

The good impression he had made on the meeting had been destroyed. Even more than the shooting-bee at the saloon, the rustler's tool damned him in the eyes of the cowmen.

"C'mon, I'm lockin' yuh up," grunted Durban, proud of his own importance. "Unbuckle yore gun-belt and drop."

It was no time to start a battle, so the Ranger let his heavy gun-belt fall to the floor and stepped out of the loop. Peewee Cort picked up the holstered Colts and hung them over his own shoulder.

"I'll see to these, Tad," he growled.

"Okay."

The sheriff roughly prodded the tall Ranger out into the darkness. The deputies and witnesses trailed along. Mayor Cort walked at Hatfield's side under the wooden awnings. Lights blinked in the saloons as they headed for the small jailhouse.

The party was still two hundred yards from the lock-up, on the bare expanse of plaza. From the shadowy flanks swept a great array of masked, hard-riding hombres. The thud of mustang hoofs was loud enough to shake the earth. The Ranger was some yards ahead of most of the deputies and witnesses, walking with long strides under the fat sheriff's shotgun, Peewee Cort and a deputy at his side.

"Watch out, Sheriff, they're after us!" the deputy suddenly yelled.

The faces of the horsemen were blurs, bandannas pulled up to glittering eyes under the low Stetsons. At their head pounded a huge hombre. The Ranger saw the reddish, shaggy hair under his big hat.

"Rescue!" bellowed the chief, spurring at the four in front. "Run for it, Jim. We'll take yuh free!"

As Tad Durban cursed hotly, the swiftly approaching riders sent a blasting volley from their Colts. Bullets kicked up dust about the four, and Peewee Cort piped a squeaking curse as a slug bit his thigh. The sheriff threw his shotgun off the Ranger and pulled a trigger, the buckshot scattering and peppering into the charging horsemen.

"Run for the jail!" shouted Hatfield, snatching his gun-belt from Cort's shoulder.

Bullets were shrieking about him as he ripped out his Colts and began shooting. He felt the sting of lead in his flesh as he zigzagged, firing back on the run, Cort limping ahead of him.

Pete Norris thirstily lifted his glass of liquor from the bar of the New York Saloon.

He had recovered from the terrible injuries received by the guns of the ruthless cattle thieves who had struck and run off the Slash E herd. But he hadn't recovered his pride. The steers were gone without a trace and he had been unable to get on the track of the rustlers.

Sue Atchinson, of the Circle 3, had intrigued the wiry young foreman. He had, in fact, fallen in love with the dainty, pretty girl. But the death of her father had stricken her, and she had been too engrossed in the funeral and mourning to notice anybody much, though she usually had a sad smile for Norris.

He had hung around the ranch, doing what he could, for three or four days. But Rooster Sprague didn't like him and made no bones about showing his aversion. Norris had come perilously close to a gunfight

77

with Rooster one evening. Not wishing to make further trouble for the unfortunate girl, he had saddled up quietly and ridden southward, still on the hunt for the Slash E herd.

After wiring the home ranch of the theft from the Warwick station, he had kept on. But it was a fruitless journey he made through a wild rangeland, and at last he had swung back north.

He hit Warwick ten minutes before the arrest of Jim Hatfield. His first stop had been the big New York Saloon, where he ordered himself a long drink. Music shrilled, dancers bobbed in the annex, visible through a wide door on one side. The long bar ran the length of the room, and there were men hanging on it, drinking. Dice were being cast at the rear, where customers sat at tables. The visiting cowmen were all at the meeting up the street.

As he was raising the glass to his dry lips, Norris' attention was attracted by two men carrying a board stretcher on which lay a still, blanketed figure. They emerged from the back rooms and came swiftly up the saloon toward the front door. Behind them strode two men, bearing a dead man between them on another plank. Pete blinked as he saw that more were coming.

"Looks like a plague," he thought, staring with open mouth.

The first stretcher passed him, the blanket-covered form stiff and inert. He saw the dead man's bearded face, but it wasn't familiar. As he watched, the second one came along. The edge of the khaki blanket was drawn up to the lips. The high-peaked sombrero lay on the motionless breast. The skin was olive, the staring eyes dark.

"White buttons!" Norris gasped.

It was a physical shock that hit him. The blanket edge acted like a mask. Imprinted permanently on his brain was the picture of what had occurred back in the canyon, where he had so closely fought with death.

"I seen him!" he muttered. "That Mex was with the gang!"

In his excitement he upset his glass. As he swung to follow the stretcher-bearers, who were heading for a flat wagon and Boot Hill to bury the dead, the roar of gunfire burst over Warwick.

Pete Norris ran outside to the porch. Quickly he placed the center of the disturbance — the bare, wind-swept plaza near the town jail. He glimpsed the large band of masked riders, the flashes of their guns punctuating the affray, saw the fleeing smaller groups of men afoot shooting back.

For a moment Pete Norris stood on the porch with others who came out to watch the swift fight. Then the leader of the masked gunnies jerked his mustang around, and a shaft of moonlight hit him full. The big black stallion was familiar to Norris, and so was that giant, particularly the gleaming red hair that stuck out wildly under his Stetson.

"It's him!" roared Pete, going for his six-gun.

He hit the ground in a single jump, ducked under the continuous hitch-rail. Betsy stood with her reins over the bar, head down as she awaited him. Leaping aboard, he jerked a rein, turned on a dime and rode hell-for-leather toward the scrap.

The four up front made the jail by the skin of their teeth and disappeared inside. The lamp was doused. From the dark window and partly open door, gunfire poured out.

Venomoulsy aware that he had stumbled upon the gang of rustlers who had taken his herd and killed his comrades, Pete Norris did a foolhardy thing. Riding straight for them, though there were seventy gunnies, he began shooting into them, yelling in defiance. He saw one fall dead from his plunging, bucking mustang.

Men were emerging from the warehouse

in which the meeting was going on, guns in hand. Shouts and confusion dominated Warwick. Customers ran out of the saloons, and the dust beat high into the warm air under the pounding hoofs.

Reverberating explosions rang out as the swift fray rose to its peak. Then the battle began to diminish in crescendo, for the band of masked men did not pause long. They rode the circle of the jail once, pouring slugs in at the openings, spattering lead against the adobe brick walls. But as citizens and stockmen began hunching up on them, they swung under the howling command of the big red-headed chief and spurted off westward from the town.

Pete Norris, gun hot in his hand, shot after them, riding in the thickly rolling dust. But bullets from behind were clipping the air too close for comfort. The men shooting after the rustlers couldn't distinguish Norris as a friend and he came to his senses, realizing only sudden death awaited him if he caught up with such a large party of gunnies.

He swerved Betsy. Riding low over the white mare, he headed south, made a wide circle and came trotting back to the plaza. The firing had ceased.

Chapter VIII
Rustlers Take Stock

A light flickered inside the jail, and the door was opened. Norris could see the sheriff's office, with its desk and wooden benches, and in the rear the bars of the cells. He recognized the burly, bald-headed Durban, to whom he had made a complaint about the loss of his steers. He also saw Mayor Cort, who had been pointed out to him when he had been in Warwick before.

With them in the jail was a tall, narrow-hipped, broad-shouldered man, calm of manner and countenance. He impressed Norris at first sight as a strong and decent waddy. Deputy Ben Walton came hustling up, limping from a wrenched ankle.

"Hey, Sheriff, we better get after 'em!" he bawled.

"Aw, we'd never catch up with 'em in the dark," grumbled Tad Durban.

Peewee Cort sank into a chair, blood showing on his hand as he brought it away from his left thigh.

"They drilled me," he said. "Reckon I better get home to bed."

The bartender from the New York, one of the witnesses who had come to identify Hatfield as the killer of de Lira, trailed in, look-

82

ing white around the gills.

"Where's them other witnesses?" growled Durban.

"They run off when the shootin' began, aimin' for cover," replied Ben Walton.

"Say, Sheriff," cried Pete Norris, throwing himself off Betsy to confront the burly, hangdog Durban, "that's the gang who rustled my herd! Remember the Slash E bunch?"

"Oh, yeah?" snapped Durban. "I'm busy to the shoulders right now, bub. I recall yore yarn, but I got a killer on my hands tonight."

He scowled toward the imperturbable, tall man who leaned against the wall. He pushed back his Stetson to scratch his bald head. He was deeply puzzled, for his prisoner had brought down two of the attackers and had got Cort and his captor into the jail in the nick of time.

"Yuh gotta listen to me," insisted Norris, growing red with anger as the sheriff refused to show any interest in him. Durban, Pete decided, was none too sharp of wits. He seemed confused, unable to call the turn. "Why, them cattle thieves that hit us and stole my herd must hang around this section! Another of their chiefs is lyin' dead on a stretcher over there at the New York Saloon. A Mex with pearl buttons on his hat. I'll never forget them eyes. I seen 'em that night the gang struck us."

"What — what's that yuh say?" demanded Peewee Cort.

"I said that dead Mex over there's a rustler shore as hell's hot. He's one of the gang that killed my pards and run off our cows."

Cowmen from the distracted meeting were crowding up. Cort forgot his wound.

"There yuh are, Durban," he crowed. "What'd I tell yuh? De Lira's a cattle thief, one of the rustlers we're after. Yuh can't hold Jim for his death!"

Tad Durban blinked, cursing under his breath. He was all mixed up.

"C'mon, we'll take a look-see," he ordered.

Everybody, including the prisoner, who hung on to his guns which had been returned by Cort, trooped over to the New York. On the wagon lay the dead, Francisco de Lira among them.

"That's the feller," insisted Norris, pointing to the Mexican. "I can swear to him."

"Well, doggone my worthless hide!" exclaimed Durban. He turned his fat bulk around, glaring at the circle of faces. "Where in blazes're them witnesses?"

But the hombres who had sought to swear

Hatfield's neck into a noose had prudently disappeared. Only the dead remained.

Norris stepped over and stuck out a hand to the tall fellow.

"Say, if yuh shot this Mex, I'd like to shake, mister," he declared earnestly. "Him and that big red-headed devil who led that gang were the bosses on the raid that nearly killed me. They laid out all my pards and took our cows."

"Yuh're Pete Norris," said Hatfield in a low voice.

"Yeah," Norris replied, astonished.

"How'd yuh know?"

"Heard tell of yuh."

Tad Durban swung on the tall hombre.

"Norris is okay, I savvy that. He says that Mex was a rustler. That clears yuh of the killin' charge, but there's still that runnin' iron. I'm gonna hold yuh till I've checked up some more. I can't figger it all. It jest don't fit. Why'd that bunch of gunnies try to snatch yuh, if yuh ain't a pard of theirs?"

"Now, look, Sheriff," drawled the self-possessed ex-prisoner, "yuh need an awful lot of convincin' on a man. I helped yuh run off that gang and I didn't kill anybody but them who needed killin'. I don't hone to pass over my guns again. I'll be around whenever yuh want me."

Durban scowled, close-set black eyes reddening as he tried to return the gray-green cool gaze of the Ranger.

"I'm the law here," he blustered, "and what I say goes!"

Sue Atchinson stepped from the crowd. Pete Norris' heart jumped as he sighted the trim young woman. He had been feeling a troubled, vague unhappiness, which he had ascribed to the loss of his men and herd. But this left him at sight of Sue. Just to look at her made him joyful.

"I believe it was all a put-up game, Sheriff, to discredit Jim Harris," said the girl. "Jim, if you're still of the same mind, I hope you won't back down on the foreman's job. The Circle Three will be proud to have you."

"Thanks, ma'am. I'm still of the same mind."

Pete stifled a jealous pang for he could not help seeing the girl's admiration for the big man, nor realizing that she knew and liked him. It was easy to imagine how a woman would fall under the spell of such a rugged, powerful man. Norris stepped forward.

"Ma'am, I'd like to help yuh, too," he said hopefully.

Her eyes were cool and she regarded Pete.

"You'll have to ask my foreman," she replied.

Pete grinned sourly, but he knew she was right. He swung to Jim Harris.

"Can I have a ridin' job with yuh? I'm a top-hand."

"Reckon I'll be glad to have yuh, Pete," drawled the tall waddy.

Pete Norris' grin lost its sourness completely. He told himself he was doing it so he could remain in the vicinity and thus hunt the rustlers. But deep in his heart he knew his real reason was to be near Miss Atchinson.

"Sheriff," said the new Circle 3 boss, "I ain't fightin' the law. On the other hand, I ain't lettin' my guns go again. Savvy? If yuh want me, yuh'll find me at the Circle Three."

He turned on his spurred heels and started away.

For a moment Norris thought Tad Durban was going to swell up and burst. As the fat officer's hand twitched toward his pistol, Pete braced for a scrap. He meant to help out the big fellow wo had partially avenged the Slash E. But Durban didn't draw. He only glared as the Ranger coolly ducked under the hitch-rail and disappeared in the shadows.

Sue Atchinson, having stood up for her

87

friend, walked back toward the meeting. Pete Norris ran after her and strolled at her side.

"I'd never have gone away, ma'am," he told her, "but Rooster Sprague didn't cotton to me. I figgered I'd make trouble for yuh if I stayed, and yuh had plenty of that."

She looked up at him and smiled.

"I'm glad you said that. I couldn't understand why you'd ridden off with hardly a thank you."

Pete Norris felt as though he were walking on clouds. The top of his Nebraska hat seemed to float.

He went back to the meeting, but took in little of what went on. He was too busy watching the pretty girl he had been unable to forget.

Warwick lay silent in the small hours of the morning. In a deserted freight car, swung off the main line on a siding beyond the cattle pens, several men met for a whispered conference. Their horses waited in the shadows outside. Only the red glow of their burning cigarettes made sharp red points of light in the interior of the car.

"We done our best to get him, Mohle," Red Frankie Guire drawled, "but he's quick as a flea and fast as lightnin' with them guns. Yuh know we couldn't stick too long, without runnin' into a big scrap with the odds ag'in us, mounted in the open like that."

"In my opinion it was a mistake to try for him that way," another said gruffly. "It should have been done quietly."

"Huh," grunted Mohle, eyes glowing with the reflected light of his cigarette as he drew deeply on it. "De Lira tried that. Damn that big jigger! You're right, Frankie, he's somethin' extra-special. I couldn't plug him, watched as I was. Besides, he's always moving, always ready."

"I'm mighty sorry to lose Francisco," stated Guire. "He was a big help to me, gents. One day I'll make that skunk who shot him pay."

"Puts me on a hot spot," complained the second hombre, "after all I said and did. He's leery of me now."

"You're right," agreed Mohle, the chief. "He's got to die. But he's a lot smarter than I thought and it must be figured right next time, boys. He's riding out to take over the Circle Three in the morning."

Mohle swung on a silent figure hunched against the freight car wall. "You go out there tomorrow and eat dirt. Savvy? Get back in there somehow."

"Who, me?" cried the fourth, starting violently. "Nope, I won't do it. I don't like that Jim jigger. He's hell and sudden death. I ain't foolin' with bear traps like him!"

Mohle cursed impatiently, took a step toward the huddled figure, who shrank from his dangerous eyes.

"You do what I tell you to do," he snarled, "or you'll find yourself playing poker in hell with de Lira. Savvy?"

"Okay, okay, Chief. I'll do it, but it's playin' with a loaded gun. That Harris ain't no plain cow-nursin' waddy."

Mohle was silent for a moment.

"If I thought he was a Ranger," he growled, "I'd lay off for awhile, till he got fed up and left the country."

"A Ranger!"

The mention of the great law organization was like a dash of ice-water to these criminals who plotted against Texas. The Rangers, they knew, were the only men who could ever bring them to book. They could beat county and town officers easily, overwhelm such meager forces, but the Texas Rangers were a different proposition.

"We'll finish him off, and that nosey Norris with him," promised Mohle confidently. "That'll end the opposition, gents. Just stand by till you hear from me, and you'll see the king of the rustlers win out."

The confidence of the chief transmitted itself to them. He was the fiercest and cleverest of them all, and under his plotting brain they had come a long way toward the realization of their greedy dreams, through his shrewdness, vast fortunes had already been torn from the heart of Texas.

CHAPTER IX
NEW FOREMAN

The brilliant sun of southwest Texas shone over the Circle 3 ranch gleaming on the flat roofs of the rambling and comfortable house, on bunkhouse and barns, over corrals in which were strong, fast mustangs. Here were all the necessities for a cattle outfit in a grassy valley. Cottonwoods grew around the waterholes, and a windmill thrust its ungainly arms to the brazen blue sky.

This, the Ranger knew, was the part of the industry which had made Texas strong. Built up from nothing by Pop Atchinson's own hard labor and brains, a paradise that had been nothing but wilderness, the Circle 3 was the very type of outfit Jim Hatfield was fighting to save from ruin at the hands of wholesale cattle thieves.

Two days before, he had been in Warwick. It had taken most of the intervening hours to ride out to the spread with Sue and Pete Norris. Now he was on duty, his first tour as the foreman of the ranch.

He looked toward the east, where the Comanches rose, a forbidding wall of rock to check all progress that way. The mountains dropped off southward, and in the invisible distance lay Warwick and the railroad. To the north the land was hilly, filled with hidden draws, covered with dense chaparral and scrub timber. To the west lay chunk prairie, covered by coarse, nutritious grasses, the best of fodder for browsing steers. In the background were more gray-brown hills.

"It's a nice spread, ain't it?" a voice said.

The Ranger swung, to see Pete Norris at his side, grinning.

"Yeah," grunted Hatfield. "Which way'd yuh say yuh was when they attacked yuh that night, Pete?"

Norris waved his hand to the north.

"Up there, camped in a blind canyon. That big redhead and de Lira struck with a powerful bunch of gunmen, Jim. I trailed down and run into Rooster Sprague and Miss Sue, stumbled on her dad, shot to death. That way" — he pointed at the steep mountains in the east — "is plumb blocked off from this range. It'd take all a man could do afoot to cross them hills. I lost the trail anyway, and I reckon my cows're beef by this time."

The handsome golden gelding, which Hatfield rode out here and which Norris had observed with admiring eyes, came strolling up and nuzzled his master's hand.

"Take it easy, Goldy," murmured the Ranger. "We'll soon get goin' again."

A pet, the sorrel was allowed to roam as he willed. He would come at a whistle from Hatfield. Goldy sniffed, snorted, stamped a hoof. The Ranger turned to look along the lane. It was empty.

"Someone's comin'," he declared.

The sorrel had told him this. After awhile they saw dust over the line of manzanita bushes along the fence. A rider on a dusty chestnut mustang swung through the gate, after opening it by the hanging stick. He closed the gates, and proceeded slowly toward the two standing by the horse corral.

Sue had let her cowboys go, before riding to Warwick to sell out to George Vane. There was only an old retainer, who cooked and tended the riding stock, besides Hatfield and Norris, on the Circle 3 at the moment.

But there would be half a dozen waddies out to resume work the following day. Hatfield and Sue had left orders in town for them.

"By golly," exclaimed Norris, "if it ain't Rooster Sprague!"

The red-faced, craw-throated, bony ex-foreman of the spread blinked nervously as he pulled his chestnut to a halt and waited for an invitation to dismount.

"Howdy," he said at last, when nobody had spoken for an embarrassingly long time.

The gray-green eyes never left the uncomfortable Sprague's thin features.

"Howdy," drawled Hatfield.

He was calculating the reason for Rooster's return. It was brazen, to say the least, for the Ranger was sure that the ex-foreman had pointed him out to de Lira at the New York Saloon that night. In addition, there was the fact that Rooster had urged Miss Atchinson to sell out to the Vane Syndicate. "I been feelin' mighty bad, mister, about the turn things've took," Rooster began in his whining voice. "I hope yuh don't hold no hard feelin's. I come out to tell yuh I was mistook when I told Miss Sue to sell the spread. I still think it'll be a hard pull, but I jest couldn't stand by without tryin' to give yuh a hand. I know the ropes here

94

and I'll work at waddy's pay under yuh, mister. In fact, if yuh don't want me at all, why, I'll be willin' to stay a few days to show yuh the main points of the spread."

"That's mighty white of yuh, Sprague," said Hatfield gratefully. "Light and rest yore legs."

"Thanks. It's a long run out from town, ain't it?"

Rooster, seeming relieved, got down and unsaddled, hanging the leather on the top rail of the corral and turning his chestnut horse into the pen. He got himself a drink at the trough and swung back to the frowning Pete Norris. Norris didn't seem pleased to see him, but Rooster was in a contrite mood. He was quite humble and there was none of that arrogance in his demeanor which had brought on trouble between Norris and him before.

"What's yore first idea, Jim?" he asked. "I'm with yuh, whatever yuh decide. I'm loyal to this here brand, even if I think it can't pay."

"How touchin'," Norris snapped.

Hatfield blinked but did not laugh.

"Yuh might go out, Rooster, and check up the gear," he suggested. "My idea is to get what steers we can together fast and sell 'em. Miss Atchinson needs cash to go on."

"Yeah, but there ain't any marketable beef. The rustlers got it all."

"Never seen country like this where yuh couldn't scrape up a hundred or more head in the draws," contradicted the Ranger. "Rustlers work fast. They can't go into all the nooks and corners. Even reg'lar riders'll miss some stuff. Ain't that so?"

"Yeah, I reckon so," agreed Rooster. "Mebbe it ain't a bad idea at that. I'll shore help."

"Good. Get goin' on that gear, will yuh? I want everything shipshape when the boys ride in tomorrer."

Rooster ambled off, like an animated pair of shears. Pete Norris frowned.

"That perambulatin' pink snake gets my dander roused every time, Jim," he said disgustedly. "I ain't got no use for him at — all."

"I figger mebbe I will have," the Ranger remarked softly.

He meant to keep a close watch on Sprague, which was why he had hired the ex-foreman. It would be easier to observe Rooster's actions by having him close at hand than roaming the range. He had no illusions about what Rooster termed his "loyalty" to the Atchinsons.

Next morning six waddies rode into the Circle 3 yard, unsaddled their horses and reported for duty to Hatfield, new foreman of the ranch.

"Norris," ordered the Ranger, "take four men and start combin' them north woods. Rooster and me'll ride with the other two and hunt the west range. We'll pool what we get in that basin, cull 'em out and later brand 'em close to home. Savvy?"

"Right, Jim."

The expert Norris and four waddies rode out of the Circle 3 a short while later. Hatfield rode the sorrel, which was a well trained cowpony. He took the west way, Sprague with him.

From a bushy mesquite ridge, after a couple of hours, they scanned the grazing sections of the spread.

"Ain't much good stuff left, mister," ventured Rooster. "Them animals over there are mossy horns, too tough to ship."

This was true enough. Whatever stock Hatfield had seen wasn't fit to eat. The cream of the Atchinson steers had been rustled. But he split his crew, sending a rider up every small draw he came to.

On Goldy he pushed slowly along a narrow, torturous trace that was hardly wide enough for a deer. Save for the humming, buzzing insects in the hot sunshine, the draw seemed deserted.

But suddenly, right under the sorrel's nose, up leaped a powerful three-year-old longhorn from his hiding bed in the chaparral. It snorted, racing with the wild rush of an escaping panther. Cunning as any jungle beast, such stock often eluded roundups for years and it was these creatures the Ranger sought now.

"Jump, Goldy!" roared Hatfield, pulling his rein.

The sorrel managed to elude the curved horn that murderously drove sideward at them as the cow went by, head down and tail up. They ran the steer out into the open and headed for the designated place of collection.

A Circle 3 waddy was already there, holding another cow. The two were shoved into a hollow to await further recruits to the herd. Both animals had been branded as calves when they were following their mothers.

All through the day the sweating men worked under the skilful guidance of Hatfield. When it was time to quit, they had forty marketable cows in the collection. Many were unbranded, proving they had escaped all previous roundups.

Pete Norris and his boys joined them, driving thirty more steers. The bunches were melded, driven toward home and penned safe in the ranch corrals.

It was long after dark when the worn-out cowboys pulled into the Circle 3 yard and went to eat.

Next morning the Ranger had them all up bright and early, before the red of the new sun tinged the sky. They started out once more, to comb new sections of the range.

Toward noon, Jim Hatfield was riding up another of the narrow, sand-floored draws. Prickly pears carpeted the earth. He flushed a strange-looking creature.

It was a cow, but she had evidently been in a fight a year or two before. She had lost one horn, and injured a hind leg, for her left pin was bent at a sharp angle and her gait was so comical that Hatfield had to grin. Besides her injuries, her coloring was different from the usual dusty hue of the longhorn. She had big white splotches on her wide flanks. Perhaps it was her individual coloring which had made other herd beasts dislike her and pick fights. Her hide was covered with horn scars. She had never been branded.

"Doggone, yuh're the funniest-lookin' critter I ever did see," the Ranger said aloud.

He headed her off and ran her into the bunch, where the other cows sniffed suspiciously, lowing at her. Once in a great while a cowboy came across such a beast. This one brought grins from the waddies when they arrived.

They didn't have the luck they had had the day before. But that night, with Norris' offering pooled, they added forty more to the bunch.

Four days after starting, Hatfield had two hundred and fifty head of prime cows, branded, earmarked and ready to sell. When they were rested and fattened a bit, he meant to drive them to Warwick and the railroad pens.

"Nice work," complimented Sue Atchinson, leaning on the fence and looking them over. "Why, with the money we get for them, Jim, I'll be able to tide over till the next batch of calves grows up!"

There was always something to do around a ranch — fence and leather mending, watering thirsty horses and steers. The Circle 3 seemed to be proceeding efficiently and quietly toward prosperity, under the skilful hand of its new boss. Rooster Sprague had been docile and willing, doing more than his share of the work.

After supper, the men repaired to their bunks to sleep, worn out from a long day's toil. Jim Hatfield went off to sleep with the others.

He started awake a few hours later. His six-gun, never far from his hand when he slept, was gripped in his long fingers. He opened his eyes, listening, wondering what had prodded his keen senses.

A pale shaft of moonlight came through the window of the bunkhouse. Snores of various calibers broke the quiet. Then he heard the distant hooting of an owl outside. Once, twice it called, a pause, and then a third. After a moment it came again.

"That's a mighty reg'lar owl," he thought, rising up on his elbows and peering around in the gloom. One of the bunks was empty. "Rooster's on the move, I reckon."

Hatfield swung his feet to the floor and quickly pulled on his boots. No doubt Sprague's stealthy exit was what had wakened him. The door was open a crack.

He slipped out into the moonlight and looked around the yard. A dark figure was silently walking toward the rise to the north, where some big cottonwoods threw deep shadows over the ground.

The owlhooting came again. Hatfield placed it among the trees.

A quick scrutiny told him that he could round the open space by cutting behind the horse corral and making a circle to get up on the grove.

Chapter X
Rustler Fury

It took some minutes to complete this maneuver. The tall Ranger moved with the soft tread of a stalking tiger. Flat on his belly when there was danger of being seen, he wormed close enough to the cottonwoods to hear what was being said.

"Why the devil ain't yuh reported?" a gruff voice demanded. "Mohle's been waitin' to hear what went on over here."

"Yuh red-haired fool," Sprague snarled angrily, "that big jigger Harris sleeps with one eye open and the other only half-closed! I been watched like a dropped calf. I'm takin' my life in my hands jest to come out here now. Yore hootin' was enough to wake the dead. He's got a herd collected and aims to drive to Warwick in a day or two. It'll save the spread for the gal. Tell the chief I ain't stickin' here much longer. Harris gives me the creeps and I think he's suspcious of me. Why, mebbe he's awake right now!"

"Keep a civil tongue in yore head," growled the big hombre to whom Sprague was talking. "Mohle's waitin' up there on the ridge, Rooster. We seen 'em drivin' steers this away and he wanted to savvy what it's all about. The chief aims to get the Circle Three, and nobody's stoppin' us. Why don't yuh run a knife between that Harris skunk's short ribs?"

"I ain't been able to get behind him. He's fast as a snake and twice as supple. I tell yuh, I ain't goin' to fiddle with that load of dynamite no longer, Guire."

"Huh," thought the listening Ranger, "Guire is a sorrel-top. Must be Red Frankie Guire. I've heard tell of that rustler. Must've been him in Warwick the other night, too!"

Besides the red-headed gunny, he had another name, "Mohle," who was given allegiance by Red Guire. From Arizona sheriffs, from Kansas and Indian Territory, had come reports on Frankie Guire. For many years there had been complaints of his cattle and horse stealing, and cold-blooded killings. Now evidently Guire had hit Texas as part of a big gang.

"Tell Mohle I'll see him at the camp day after tomorrer," said Rooster. "I'm headin' back now."

Hatfield strained his eyes toward the razorback ridge to the right. He could see nothing there save the blackness of shadow chaparral. From the corral came the lowing of the steers he had got together by such hard work, to save the Circle 3 for Sue Atchinson. He had another purpose in his endeavor, desiring to familiarize himself with the neighborhood and discover why the Vane Syndicate seemed so anxious to get control of the ranch.

He began to creep back, aware that Sprague was soon going to leave Guire. Rooster was in a tremendous hurry, however. Cursing down Guire's objections, he swung and padded swiftly toward the bunkhouse.

For an instant Hatfield glimpsed the giant form. Red Frankie Guire emerged from the cottonwoods, threw a leg over a black stallion and galloped off toward the ridge.

Rooster Sprague, headed in a straight line, reached the door before the Ranger, and cautiously opened it. Jim Hatfield was a yard behind him. The lean hombre turned and saw that the big Ranger had him. "I knowed it —" Sprague blurted, then broke off, his teeth chattering. He said hysterically: "I was feelin' sick and stepped out to get some cool water, Harris."

Hatfield caught him by the throat.

"Yuh've cooked yore own hash, Rooster," he growled. "From now on yuh're doin' jest what I say or I'll ventilate yore worthless carcass. Savvy? I want Mohle and Red Guire and that rustler gang yuh work for!"

"Cut it out," squeaked Sprague, in a dither of terror. "I'll — I'll do anything yuh tell me! Don't kill me!"

"Good."

Hatfield relaxed his pressure, pleased with the success of his ruse in letting Sprague remain at the Circle 3. He had hoped that sooner or later he would gain valuable information by watching Rooster. Now he had an inside member of the cattle thieves broken and ready to obey.

The Ranger, keeping a loose hold on his prisoner, reached around and extracted the six-shooter from Sprague's belt. He could feel Rooster shaking with terror.

"Who's this chief of yores, the one named Mohle?" Hatfield demanded.

Sprague started, and his teeth rattled together like dry bones in a box.

"Mohle?" he stammered. "Mohle?" Hatfield shook him violently, putting on threatening pressure. Rooster cried: "He's the

105

King of the Rustlers! He's after the Circle Three and he made me come here. Honest, I was forced to work for 'em —"

"What the hell's goin' on?" a sleepy voice cut in — from a nearby bunk.

One of the waddies, Shorty Burns, had roused up. He struck a match and reaching out, touched it to the blackened wick of a lantern standing on a crate close to his bed.

"Douse that light, Shorty," commanded Hatfield.

"What's up?" asked the surprised Shorty, slow to comply. "What's wrong with Rooster? Looks like he'd seen a ghost."

"Put that light out," repeated the Ranger, starting for it. Just as he moved, a gun roared from the open narrow window at the rear of the bunkhouse. The bullet burned fiercely as it seared Hatfield's side, cutting a furrow in the flesh and smashing him to his knees. Echoes of the shot banged in the confined space of the bunkhouse. The rest of the men, rousing up, stared open-mouthed at the ambush in the night.

With a spasmodic movement, the Ranger forced his long body behind the end of a bunk. Another slug threw up dirt from the bare earthen floor of the building.

Someone was gunning for him from the window. He sought to draw his Colt. It was pinned under his thigh and he had to shift to get it out. In the intervening instants, Rooster Sprague stood frozen where he was, eyes wide as saucers, brimming over with horror.

"No — don't, Mohle! I ain't squealin' —"

The gawky waddy, red face working, Adam's apple jumping, realized even before the Ranger what his fate was to be. He saw the black rifle muzzle swinging on himself.

As Hatfield shifted and drew his hogleg, Rooster Sprague was whirled around by the force of a bullet that drilled his head from forehead to back. He went down hard, his legs kicking in sheer nervous reflex. Then he stiffened out on the floor, motionless in death.

Hatfield fired an instant later at the window. The rifle barrel was already being withdrawn. He thought he heard, in the ear-dinning explosions, the sharp curse of a man out there. To give himself a chance to move without being seen, he sent a slug into Shorty's lamp and extinguished it.

Pete Norris fired from his bunk at the window. The cowboys began leaping up, grabbing their pistols, ready to help their foreman.

"After 'em!" shouted Hatfield.

He ran outside. The thud of hoofs reached

his ears, even as he rounded the long oblong building on the trail of the murderer.

There were half a dozen of them, bunched as they fled from the Circle 3. One was huge as a giant. He guessed it must be Red Frankie Guire. The others were only dark blurs, low over their mustangs as they sped off.

Hatfield whistled shrilly. Firing after them in the hope of making a lucky hit on the swift-moving, distant riders, he waited until Goldy came loping up to him. He mounted bareback, shouting back orders to Norris and the others to saddle up and follow.

Low over the handsome gelding's mane, the Ranger rode out after the killers. Mohle, he knew, must be among them. The king of the rustlers had tried to kill him that night. Failing, he had made certain that Sprague wouldn't betray him.

"A plumb cunnin' sidewinder," mused Hatfield.

Slowly but surely he picked up distance on the fleeing gang. Several hundred yards to his rear came Pete Norris, and then the Circle 3 waddies, strung out according to their mounts' speeds.

Mohle, the Ranger figured, had been given the report of Rooster Sprague's interview with Red Guire. From his eyrie on the ridge, perhaps he had glimpsed the Ranger trailing Sprague. He had been smart enough to sneak in to listen. When Shorty struck that light, he had sought to insure his own safety by killing Rooster, after missing Hatfield.

Across uneven ground, gun in hand as he waited to get near enough for a fair shot, the Ranger urged the swift golden horse. The rustlers had swung northeast and cut through a narrowing part of the valley. They rode in the open under the moonlight for a quarter of a mile. Hatfield was in revolver shot distance when they hit the other end of the narrows. He threw up his Colt, took aim at the black figure in the rear, and let go.

The hombre threw up both arms, straightened in agony and plunged off his horse. The animal ran on after the group, who turned in alarm. The Ranger saw the yellow-blue flashes of their spurting Colts, heard the whistling bullets about his low-bent head. Then he heard their loud shouts.

The gang was slowing, and he almost rode to his death. For there appeared, coming to meet Mohle, Guire and the handful who had been at the Circle 3 — a great band of mounted, masked hombres. Bandannas up, Guire and Mohle swung. A heavy fusillade of lead drove back at the Ranger. He swerved the golden sorrel and swung in a quick circle, his Colt spitting defiance through the night.

"Too many to handle," he muttered. "I need cover."

He galloped back the way he had come, soon meeting Pete Norris.

"There's fifty or sixty, mebbe more, headin' this way," he warned. "Git back to the ranch pronto. We gotta protect it."

Guns blasting, they rode hell-for-leather in retreat, picking up the Circle 3 waddies en route. The furious bandits, egged on by Red Frankie Guire and Mohle, king of the rustlers, pressed closely on their heels, shooting volleys after them. Hatfield sought to hold them and slow the pursuit with his accurate Colts. A lucky shot took Shorty Burns in the back, between the shoulder-blades. The waddy died as he rode for home.

The Ranger's revolver spat back revengeful slugs at the line of masked, slavering devils seeking his blood. He knocked another one from his saddle. His tearing lead, zipping too close for comfort, achieved his purpose. The rustlers were compelled to spread out and slow in pursuit.

But Mohle and his right-hand man, Red

Frankie Guire, seemed determined to finish him off this time, even if they had to take the entire Circle 3 to hell along with the Ranger. Doggedly they kept on the trail of the handful of waddies, who finally swept into the ranch-yard and leaped from their sweated leather.

There was a lamp lighted in the house. Sue Atchinson had been startled awake by the blaring shots and yells.

"Make for the house!" roared the Ranger. "Grab yore rifles and don't let 'em come close!" He left the sorrel. "Keep away from 'em, Goldy," he warned, and started the gelding off with a gentle slap, out of harm's way.

Picking up his Winchester from inside the bunkhouse, he ran for the ranchhouse, driving the men ahead of him. Miss Atchinson stood inside the front entry, her eyes anxious and alarmed.

"What is it?" she cried. "I heard the shots."

"Trouble, rustlers," Hatfield replied tersely. He strode to the table and turned out the lamp. "Norris, take that east winder. Buck, grab the west. I'll cover the front. Miss Sue, you keep down, away from doors and winders."

He disposed his fighters strategically to protect every possible position. Then he peered out from the window near the door, which he bolted. He saw the big array of masked cattle thieves come pounding up, spreading out in a fast-riding circle to pour shots into all the windows without exposing themselves long in one spot.

This was a gang that had learned well from the trickiest Indians. The Ranger knew he had ridden into a rustler plot that was far cleverer than any he had ever encountered. Getting out alive would seem a victory — but Hatfield wanted more than mere life. He wanted nothing less than the complete destruction of the rustler crew!

CHAPTER XI
HONEST REINFORCEMENTS

Hatfield, at a corner of his loophole, thrust his rifle through under the sash. He took aim and fired. He had the satisfaction of seeing a rustler drop his reins and ride sagging from the ring.

"Get in there and kill 'em!" Red Guire was bellowing to his men.

They kept moving furiously in a circle as rifles from the house spat into their lines. They couldn't do more than fire at the flashes of the defenders' guns, and the Circle 3 waddies were better shots than they cared to battle. They kept edging off, making the radius of the circle wider, despite the urging of their bosses.

Pete Norris was taking excellent care of his window, quickly pumping his Winchester. The other waddies were joking and laughing as they triggered with deadly effectiveness.

For twenty minutes the mad war raged. Hundreds of slugs struck inside or against the house. A rifle cracked behind Hatfield. From the corner of his eye he saw Sue Atchinson, gun against her slim shoulder, taking part in the defense.

"She shore has nerve," he mused. "She's a fine girl."

"We musta hit a dozen of 'em, Jim!" gloated Norris, pausing to wipe sweat from his forehead. Suddenly Pete saw the girl's rifle and he gasped. "Yuh mustn't! A stray might hit yuh!"

"They're fadin' off," Hatfield announced.

The masked rustlers were swinging off to the north. Hatfield, making sure the coast was clear, slipped outside and trailed past the bunkhouse.

"Doggone 'em!" he growled. "They're after our steers!"

The killers were at the big corrals, where the precious herd was penned.

Hatfield gave a shrill whistle and Goldy galloped to him, mane and tail flying in the wind of speed. The tall Ranger sprang aboard. Powerful legs clinching, he rode over to the house, sang out to Pete Norris on the porch.

"Get yore boys mounted. They're after the steers!"

Guns fresh-loaded, he rode madly for the corrals in which were the precious Circle 3 animals. A few of the rustlers had slipped leather and were taking the bars out. The others prepared to ride in, round the steers into a compact bunch, and drive them off.

But Hatfield's flying bullets diverted their attention. His lead hunted them, too accurate to be ignored. They dared not stay in one spot with the Ranger Colts blasting them. In wolfish fury they whirled to shoot back at the galloping phantom.

Norris and the cowboys had grabbed mustangs from the pen on the other side of the house. They rode to reinforce him, guns roaring in the moonlight.

"Pete!" called Hatfield, riding back to speak to the young waddy. "I'm goin' to start the cows millin' so's to force them skunks outa the corral. Keep 'em busy."

While Norris and his helpers fought a clever, running scrap, the Ranger streaked

114

round to the east. The cows were frightened by the banging of so many guns, maddened by the scent of acrid smoke in the night air. Hatfield increased their fright with shrill yelps, sending a barrage of bullets whistling over the groups of big steers.

The din he set up stampeded the terrified, confused steers. Cows threw up their tails, put down their heads and began to run, stumbling blindly against one another. The handful of thieves in there with them had to beat a quick retreat to keep from being crushed against the fence rails.

The tall man on the golden sorrel seemed to be everywhere at once. Cursing rustlers felt the burning lead he threw into them, and they had already had a bellyful of his fighting ability. Besides, there was a faint gray streak of the new dawn coming up over the Comanches.

Norris and the others, stubbornly fighting, were pushed back to the ranchhouse. Dismounting, they ran inside, began to shoot once more from the fortlike building. Hatfield, on the fast sorrel, stayed out, running in and out, stinging the rustlers without offering a target for their slugs.

"They've had a-plenty for tonight, Goldy," he muttered.

In the darkness to the southeast, he paused to reload his hot Colts. The rustlers, abandoning the mass of steers running wild in the pens, had to give up hope of further revenge. They swung and started away to the north, Mohle and Red Frankie Guire in the van.

Jim Hatfield, staying on their trail for half a mile to make sure they were on their way, finally quit and rode back to the ranch. Norris had closed the bars that had been pulled down. Only a few cows had escaped.

"We beat 'em, Jim!" cried Pete triumphantly.

The Ranger shook his head gravely.

"Drove 'em off for the time bein'," he growled. "But I reckon they'll be back. They're shore set on havin' this spread. One thing's certain, Pete. We can't stick here any longer."

"Huh? What yuh mean?"

"Too many of them skunks. They didn't even have their whole gang along tonight. They'll be back, I'll bet yuh a thousand to one."

"We'll drive 'em off again," Norris declared confidently.

Hatfield's somber eyes studied the exhausted waddies of the Circle 3. There wasn't one who wasn't bleeding from a flesh wound. A valuable rifleman had taken a bullet through the shoulder that incapacitated his right arm.

"What do you figure on doing, Jim?" asked Sue, her voice worried. She had come out, rifle in her small hands, to join them. "I don't want to see you boys killed, just to protect this herd."

"The ranch ain't safe for yuh, ma'am," Hatfield said soberly. "It's worse'n I figured. We'll hafta leave for awhile, till things get straightened out some. I can't stick here all the time. We'll hafta drive this herd to Warwick and sell it. Then yuh'll be able to come back here and start up again before long, when we've settled them rustlers' hash."

"All right," agreed the girl. "What you say goes, Jim."

"It's a good idea," Norris stated. "I don't feel comfortable havin' Miss Sue out here, either. She'll be better off in town."

"We'll get that herd started right now," ordered Hatfield, "and drive south. We oughta make Warwick in four days easy."

The Circle 3 crew paused for hot coffee and a bite to eat. Then, as the gray dawn dropped over the valley, the herd calmed down a bit, tired enough to be handled. The

117

men of the ranch, accompanied by Miss Atchinson, headed south, driving the steers before them.

Hatfield rode the point, on the east, off to one side. Norris was on the other point. Four flankers attempted to hold the lines of cows, slowly ambling in bunches behind their leaders. In the drag came the others, swallowing the raised dust.

By the time the sun had lost its redness and turned yellow, the entire outfit had dropped down behind a rise. Sue Atchinson, on her paint horse near the Ranger, could no longer see her beloved home when she turned to look back. Running cows was slower than riding a horse, for the creatures invariably insisted on stopping to graze, to drink, to meander about. Steers couldn't be driven too fast without ruining them and running off all fat, making their market value drop alarmingly.

These still retained much of their wildness, and there was a good deal of trouble keeping them in line.

Hatfield, on the sorrel, was constantly working to hold the point, forced to dodge back attempted escapers. He paused to mop his sweating forehead for a moment, after turning back for the twelfth time the splotched animal with the missing horn and injured leg.

"Hell," he complained to Pete Norris. "That's the funniest-lookin' steer I ever saw, and it makes more trouble than the whole herd."

"Yuh want me to shoot her or drive her off?"

"No. We'll handle 'em all. Need every head we can get."

At a creek, the cattle spread out to drink. They hated to leave the water and it took two hours to line them out and cross them into driving formation again.

The first day out they made fifteen miles, and camped for the night, for the cows had to graze and rest.

Late in the afternoon of the second day, they were twenty-five miles from the Circle 3 in the meandering line the steers had picked. Hatfield, riding the van, sighted a large band of horsemen cutting their trail.

"Looks like more trouble," he warned, hand dropping to his gun.

There were thirty or more riders in the band. They showed quick interest in the Circle 3 party as they sighted the cloud of dust, topping a ridge to the southeast of the herd.

In the distance a gun popped, echoing over the rolling, bushy land. The whole pack of horsemen swung from their course, which was to the northwest, and headed toward the Ranger. Hatfield raised his hand, making Norris and the rest rapidly check the onward progress of the bunch.

"Guns ready," he commanded.

There wasn't any cover near and he spurred out, alert for attack, peering at the hombres who had come from the direction of Warwick. But as the big Ranger, dust coating him from the drive, drew closer, he recognized several of the men.

There was Sheriff Tad Durban, burly and solid in his saddle. Brant Tazewell, new president of the Brewster County cattlemen. Ben Walton, and a bony fellow Hatfield knew as "Slim" Green, both deputies of Walton. Drew Perry, the stockman from the Panhandle. A couple of dozen ranchers, cowboys and townsmen rode in an armed band behind these leaders.

"Howdy, gents," Hatfield sang out.

He was relieved to see they were honest citizens and not Red Guire's gang of rustlers. He held his hand high in peaceful greeting. As he shoved the sorrel close, he was aware of Durban's scowling eyes upon him. Obviously the sheriff still held him in suspicion. Brant Tazewell grinned at him, spurring his horse out to greet him.

"Why, hello, Jim! Ain't that Miss Atchinson over there?"

"Shore is," drawled the Ranger, cocking a leg around his saddle horn to rest comfortably while he rolled himself a quirly.

"Them her animals?"

"Yep."

"Huh. Glad to see she found some to drive. When we first spotted yuh, we thought yuh might be the thieves we're after."

"So yuh're on the prod, huh?"

"Shore," replied Tazewell. "We took yore advice, mister. We put out patrols to watch the range for the rustlers, kept a band of fightin' men in Warwick ready to ride out quick at the first alarm. And it come. The O Bar V to the northwest reported they lost two hundred head and we're on our way."

"Good. I reckon I'll ride with yuh."

"Glad to have yuh."

Hatfield swung the sorrel and rode back to Pete Norris.

"Take the herd from here on out, Norris," he ordered. "I got important business to tend to. Yuh're halfway there now and ought to make it without trouble. But it'd be better if yuh sent Miss Sue to Warwick direct. Yuh kin spare a man to ride with her. Start her in the mornin', and she'll be safe by night."

"Okay," Norris agreed.

Tazewell, Durban and their friends were in a hurry, hoping to intercept the stolen herd from the O Bar V. Hatfield fell into line with them.

They rode on northwest, quickly leaving the Circle 3 steers behind on their way to Warwick. There wasn't much light left. The country rose in slow steps, broken by ravines and woods.

"Reckon we better camp for the night," suggested Tazewell. "Cain't see nothin' in the dark. We might pass them skunks without knowin' it."

On a high spot, they dismounted as the sun dropped behind the far-off mountains. Swiftly they set about eating.

"There's a fire over there!" cried Walton suddenly.

"Shore enough," grumbled Durban.

In the new darkness, the small red glow was visible. It came from a wooded hillside about a mile to the west of their position.

"Ten to one it's our men," said Tazewell. "Let's go, boys. Check yore guns."

Hurriedly they resaddled. Guns ready, they started single-file along a narrow cattle trail that wound up through the timber toward the spot where the fire acted as a directing beacon. Eager to come to grips with the rustlers who had so harassed their range, the cowmen pushed on.

Chapter XII
One-Sided Battle

A path wound up through a twisting, steep-walled gulch toward the site of the fire. Tazewell got the posse together, and in a low voice gave his commands.

"We'll leave our hosses down here and creep up on foot. They're prob'ly sleepin'. Keep quiet as yuh can and muzzle yore broncs."

Each man tied his bandanna around the muzzle of his mustang to prevent any whinnying alarm. Three were left to hold the bunches of reins, and the avengers started up through the deep, red-walled cut. Hatfield toted his Colts in holster, his lariat slung across one shoulder for use in climbing, if need be.

It was slow going. Sharp rocks imbedded in the sandy, crumbling dirt made it difficult to proceed silently at any speed.

"Why'd anybody make a camp up here?" he wondered.

His natural caution made him wary. So

far he had followed Tazewell and the sheriff. Durban obviously was still suspicious, not trusting him. He would take part in any battle against the rustlers. He was among the leaders and he paused till Tazewell came up.

"Wait here," he whispered. "Let me make shore of 'em."

"No. They might escape. Let's get on."

Tazewell was excited and pushed along up. Hatfield didn't see Durban. The fat hombre was clumsy and lagged at the rear of the line. Strung out, they felt a way along in the dim streak of moonlight that filtered into the cut.

The gulch was growing even thinner. The Ranger and Tazewell paused at a hairpin turn, down under bulging bluffs, wide enough for only one man at a time. A wind moaned in the torturous scrub mesquite and the sharp-tipped stones lining the lips of the ravine. The ribbon of sky, spattered with milky stars above them, was shadowed by scudding cloud shapes.

"Look out!" the Ranger warned. Leaping back, he carried Brant Tazewell with him. A scraping, grinding noise was repeated behind them, and thudding crashes split the air. A bright train of yellowish flame with a violet, licking tongue swished down the rocks. With a *whoosh* it took hold on a pile of dry rubble, leaves and sticks on a flat rock to the side. In the illumination of the bonfire, set off by a powder train and ignited swiftly by gunpowder mixed with the tinder, they saw they were covered by rifles thrust from both edges of the gulch. Boulders smashed down, pinning them.

"Throw down yore guns and reach!" a gruff voice snarled.

They had walked into a trap. Only the Ranger at once realized that the grinding, thudding boulders, poised above on a hair-trigger and then shoved into the narrow cut to block their escape, had them pinned in a death trap.

They had been strung out as they carefully climbed up, so not all the party had been caught in the space between the dropped rocks. Sheriff Durban, among the ten others at the rear, had escaped being blocked in there. Confused yells came from them.

Hatfield instantly went into action. Tazewell, with a curse, threw up his pistol and fired at a Stetson top he glimpsed above. In reply, the carbines rattled, and two of the posse took lead. The rest went milling around, wildly hunting a way out. The whole scene was lit up by the bonfire.

Hatfield was aware that only seconds remained before they all must surrender or die. He stooped, crushed against one side of the rock wall, digging into the sandy red soil with his long hands.

Scooping up the loose sand caused by erosion from the steep walls, he hurled it over the fire. He knew the enemy could see the men down there while they themselves were in shadow.

As he flung several handfuls into the licking flames, heavy smoke began pouring up, so that the light grew less bright. Guns were flashing. A man screamed in agony as a slug of death caught him in the chest.

The swift Ranger, seeking instants in which to get a fighting chance for life, refusing to surrender, kicked more dirt onto the flames. They were only phantoms now, hunting for air through the sand he had flung on. The dense volume of smoke that rolled up screened the men in the gulch and half-blinded the dry gulchers who sought to pick them off.

Bullets were snapping on the rocks, plugging into the sandy dirt about the tall Ranger. But he moved like a wraith, taking the lariat from his shoulder. He made a cast, loop wide, and it caught around the scrubby mesquite limbs. After cautiously trying it, he pulled himself up through the thick smoke that acted as a cloak in the night. His eyes watered and smarted from the vapor, but he knew the enemy must be blinded, too.

He seized the precious breaths of time to make the top.

He pulled himself flat over the brim, drew his Colt, the hammer thrown back under his thumb. A half dozen feet from him he saw, through a vista of wreathing smoke, masked hombres peering toward him with slitted, blearily watering eyes. He raised his hogleg, took aim and let go. A rustler toppled into the cut. Mouth a grim, straight line, teeth gritted, the tall Ranger inched himself along the edge of the trap cut, ripping into the flanks of the foe with his terrible lead. All was confusion in the rising smoke. The fire was about gone, doused by the dirt he had thrown on it, the powder all exploded. Frenzied men were all about him as he moved, his revolvers busy. He was able to aim at the flashes he saw as the killers blindly sought to wreak their havoc among the trapped posse below.

Blood streamed from his cuts and creases, but no slug had hit a vital spot. He realized that there were not more than twenty-five or thirty of the gunnies on both sides, and he had already thinned out the flank he was attacking.

Tazewell and his men had got their breath, caught their wits after the first panic. They had been afforded this opportunity by the Ranger's swift play. They had reached the jumbled rocks to the rear and were helping one another up and over.

Jim Hatfield had been in many a tight spot. This one had been so close that he had kissed the cold lips of death. Unwilling to desert his friends, he was fighting to pull them out of there. His bullets were throwing confusion into the enfiladed line on his side. The survivors jumped up, started backing away from his snarling guns.

He crouched in a rock nest occupied a few moments before by the dead rustler beside whose body he knelt. The Ranger began shooting through the thinning smoke at the flashes from the carbines on the opposite bank.

"Durban!" he roared, his voice booming over the din of the battle. "Get yore men up on the west bluff pronto, and drive them skunks off!"

He could hear the yells and shots that came from the sheriff's party, which had been too far behind to enter the trap. Sweating, fighting hombres sought one another in the darkness. Given a break by the Ranger, Tazewell's men put up a brave resistance. The Ranger's guns, hot in his slim hands, turned the tide, and the fire from the brink of the gulch slackened. With relief he recognized Brant Tazewell's stentorian bellowing to his right. He figured the cowmen's chief must be outside the trap. The resistance to the attackers seemed to be increasing steadily. Over on the other side, guns were screaming and flashing up, slowly approaching the ambushers.

"I'd shore like to take some of these rustlers prisoner," muttered Hatfield. "If I could get some of 'em to talkin', it'd be a big help. I wonder where the main part of Red Guire's gang is, though."

It was plain that only a section of the cattle thieves' great array of gunnies was present at the ambush. Had it not been for Hatfield's presence, the force would have been ample to annihilate the ranchers. But the terrific fighting ability of the Ranger had swung the pendulum the other way. Though the battle was still raging, it was no longer one-sided. The blinding smoke created by the quick-thinking Hatfield had screened the cowmen for the vital moment they needed to pull themselves together.

The heavy crackle of brush and sliding

stones forced him to turn. Several of the rustlers had reformed back in the chaparral and were heading his way, guns going full blast. Lead spattered about his rocks, or ricocheted off across the gulch into the night.

His face was streaked with bloody, sweated dust and powder smoke, the Stetson chin strap taut under the strong line of his fighting jaw. The Ranger shoved fresh shells into his cylinders and, flat in the rocks, returned these tokens with interest.

He could see their dark forms, the blurs that were masked faces, coming at him. Spurting six-shooters snarled for his life, lead hunting his heart and brain.

Pete Norris sighed with relief. Night had fallen over the rolling hills, northwest of Warwick. This was the last night, he figured, that he would be out with Miss Sue Atchinson's Circle 3 bunch. He had lost only one cow, a mossy-horned, fast-running steer that had eluded the cowboys in the darkness of the previous night.

With the cash she would get for the steers, Sue Atchinson could hold out a year, perhaps more, while her new calves grew to market size.

"We'll have these critters in the railroad

pens by dark tomorrer, boys," declared Norris as they fried themselves some dried beef strips and boiled a pot of coffee.

Eastward, the tall pine and bush-clad slopes of the Comanches blocked the way. They dropped off to the south, however, and in the gap ran the railroad beside which stood Warwick. For mile after mile the Comanches held their lines, keeping men and animals from crossing their fastnesses.

The velvet night, a breeze springing up with the sunset, fell over them like a vast blanket. The steers, having been driven for three days, were broken to the trail and weary from the long walk. For the time being they were willing to graze and not stampede whenever a man sneezed.

As for Norris, he wrapped himself in his blanket after a smoke. With his head on the saddle, he dropped off to sleep, dreaming of a slim, blue-eyed, golden-haired young woman.

He roused after some hours. The moon was up, and from its position and the stars he guessed it was around midnight.

"Hey, Norris!" called Billy Frisch, one of the Circle 3 waddies who had been doing night herd duty.

Frisch rode up and dismounted, squatted by his side.

"What's wrong, Billy?" demanded Norris, rising quickly.

"Dunno. Sounds like a big herd a-comin' our way. It's likely to sweep up our critters."

Norris, pulling on his boots, paused and listened. On the night, from the south, came a low rumble, that sounded like thunder. But he knew it was the pounding and trampling of a great mass of swiftly approaching cattle.

"Rouse up, boys!" he shouted.

The Circle 3 men leaped to action. Boots were yanked on hurriedly, saddles grabbed. They ran with bowlegged stride to the pen, which had been made by looping lariats about sticks pounded deep in the ground. Inside the improvised pen their mustangs stood. No properly trained horse would try to break through any kind of corral.

"Get them dogies rollin' west, outa the way!" roared Pete Norris, in his saddle. "There's a big dip a couple miles over. Seen it yesterday. We'll head for it —"

"Here they come!" cut in Frisch, whirling his horse on a dime and galloping south.

The thunder of hoofs had increased to an ominous earthshaking roar. Under the silvery moonlight, Pete Norris saw the van of the cattle herd coming, dust rolling high up into the air under the driving hoofs.

"Blast 'em," he cursed. "They must be loco, runnin' steers thataway."

The Circle 3 waddies sought to move their herd out of the direct route of the approaching stampede. Dark figures of flankers on one edge of the other herd loomed in the darkness. Their bandannas were up, but Pete thought that was because of the dust.

He was totally engrossed in preventing the Circle 3 bunch from mingling with the running, blinded cows that were almost upon them. After getting the unwieldy animals into motion westward, he was beating the rumps of the leaders with his Nebraska hat.

"Dawggone stubborn critters," he grumbled, for the steers, usually ready to run in every direction, were too slow for him now.

Gunshots blasted from the horsemen of the other outfit. Wild shrieks urged on the running, maddened steers in the big herd.

Norris grew suspicious. These might be rustlers, Red Guire's bunch. But they were coming up on a line that would have brought them dangerously close to Warwick.

"Not if the sheriff and that patrol was out," he thought, recalling the fact that many of the protectors there had ridden off northwest.

To the south, across the railroad, lay

several large spreads — the U No, the Running J. These cows might have been rustled from them. . . .

Chapter XIII
Captured

Dust from beating hoofs obscured his vision. He was aware that the breast of the swiftly approaching herd was dangerously close, the long-horned heads lowered. Such beasts could disembowel a cowpony and trample the rider to death.

He whipped out his gun, fired into the faces of the leaders. Several swerved, but the crush behind was too great, and they kept coming on. A couple were knocked sprawling, then trampled to death by their blinded mates. More shots and warwhoops came from the practically invisible drivers, hidden on the flanks and in the drag dust.

Norris realized it was impossible to make the safety of the west edge of the other herd. There were too many plunging, mighty steers upon them. The beasts had come up too suddenly upon the sleeping Circle 3.

"Curse their hides!" gritted Norris, cold sweat upon his brow.

Upon his subconscious mind was the horrible scar of another night, when he had awakened to terror and the awful massacre of his friends. The close shave with death for himself had been terrifying, but it was the loss of his Slash E herd which had cut his pride to the quick. The same emotions now battled through him and he was trembling with the same helpless rage he had experienced before.

The charging line of steers, great horns sharp as stilettos and backed by a thousand or more pounds of solid muscle, bristled within a few yards of him. A wall of dust rose to hide the bulk of the big herd in murderous obscurity, but the thundering in his ears and long years of training, warned him of the inevitable fatal impact. Once they struck Norris' horse, he knew he was as good as dead. But he had faced death before, and the desire to save Sue's pitiful bunch was stronger than the instinct of self-preservation. If his attempt were successful, it would mean survival for the Circle 3 — Sue's survival.

Betsy, the white and pink-spotted mustang mare he rode, was a trained cowpony. She knew far too much to be overrun while she still had her legs under her. At the very last instant, she swerved and ran like a deer in front of the stampeding herd.

The Circle 3 animals, bellowing with

alarm as the great herd swept up, swung to run. Some were knocked sprawling, but most of them turned and took up the mad race, stampeding for all they were worth, tails up and heads down.

The impact of huge bodies was a constant noise in the confused, thunderous din.

Ahead of the running steers, trying to divert the stampede by angling whenever possible, young Pete Norris galloped. As he looked back, he could see the dangerous longhorns always pressing upon the pretty mare's flanks. Betsy knew it was life or death for them both. If she chanced to put a hoof into a gopher hole or some other irregularity and went down, that would be the end.

For three miles, rapidly losing the distance he had made in his careful drive to conserve the beef on the Circle 3 bunch, Pete Norris kept going, ever edging for the outside of the big herd. The wild longhorns would drive thus for hours, he knew, and they could run nearly as fast as a mustang.

He was aware that there were horsemen out on the flanks, and there must be some behind to keep the cows moving in such a straight course. The Circle 3 herd was running along with the bigger group. As he looked back once, Pete saw the comical, queer-gaited steer among the leaders — the one-horned clown which had so amused his friend Jim.

Many a cowboy had died in a night stampede, his horse breaking through the thin crust and throwing its rider. Or, in the blinding dust, many had gone over the edge of some deep ravine, to be crushed under hundreds of tons of falling steers.

"Wonder where the other boys are," Norris muttered, coughing dust from his dry throat.

On they swept northward, and Pete continued making distance so that he would finally be able to flank the charging stampede. Betsy ran magnificently, picking her way almost with daintiness, seeming to test each chunk of prairie wood sod before she trusted it with her weight.

"Good girl," Norris said, patting her sweated neck.

His leather creaked under him, cinches straining over the powerful muscles of the flying mustang. A rider from the time he could toddle, only one disaster could shake Pete Norris loose — the death or fall of his mount.

With relief he realized he was near the left flank of the big herd. The steer line was thinning out. With a final desperate spurt,

137

racing at a sharp angle northwest, Betsy made it, carrying him to safety outside the comparatively straight line of the death drive.

It was a sudden, strange relief from the interminable drumming confusion out in front of the longhorns. Norris sought to turn, but the entire flank of the herd was covered by driving horsemen, thick as fleas, pounding along, keeping the steers in line.

They might be decent waddies, seeking to stop the run by letting the cows run themselves out, but Norris was suspicious of them. He kept his six-shooter ready in his hand.

"That's one of 'em!" roared a giant hombre, raising a hand to point him out. "Get him. It's that Norris skunk!"

"That's Red Frankie Guire!" gasped Pete.

Norris had had no chance to get his breath after his close shave with the trampling herd. He threw up his pistol, firing at them as he spurred Betsy west, seeking escape. One of them went down, plunging clear of his saddle. The mustang went dashing on. But there were too many of them coming at full-tilt and the instants ticked off without bringing safety.

Betsy was trying to clear them in vain. When she almost made it, the giant chief

138

began roaring curses. He poured bullets at the white horse. His men swerved, following suit. Norris' six-gun spat again, but the jolting pace was terrific, spoiling his hasty aim.

Suddenly Betsy, going hell-for-leather once more, faltered. Before he could bring up her head, she crashed on her forelegs, rolling over and over in the grassy dirt. Bullets had found her, killed her as she made her final run in the attempt to save her master. By valiant efforts she had brought him safe out of the stampede, only to be slain by the murderous guns of the rustler horde.

Norris managed to get one foot clear of his tapped stirrup. But the other, before he could disengage, his toe was caught. It yanked him around in the air as he jumped for it. Then his second boot came free, but too late to land running. He crashed heavily on his side, and a streak of pain slashed through his ribs. All the breath was knocked out of him. He was dazed, unable to move, paralyzed for moments.

Black figure after black figure, Stetsons nicked with the double triangular marks Hatfield had noted, whirled upon him. The giant hombre flung from saddle, leaped upon Norris and began beating him over the head with his Colt barrel.

Norris tried to fight, but he was unable to do so. Sudden blackness descended upon him. For the second time, the rustlers had him. The bitterness of defeat hurt more than the blows. His shame and rage were the last emotions he felt.

When Norris came to, his side ached. Needles of pain flashed through him and he thought he had cracked a couple of ribs in his fall. One arm was numb and his head ached splittingly. His broken scalp was thickly crusted with blood. He couldn't see anything at all. A jogging movement kept stirring his hurts.

He quickly realized that he wasn't blind, as he had thought in his wakening confusion. He was blindfolded by a tight cloth that was tied at the back of his head.

His head hung down, the blood throbbing in it, so he knew he was slung over the back of a horse. The familiar hairy hide was pressing his face. He could smell the animal, feel it, hear the breathing and heart-beat, and the clatter of hoofs on rocky shale. His hands were secured behind him, as were his ankles. He was hogtied and helpless as a baby.

"Mohle figgers that Atchinson female's sweet on Norris," he heard a gruff voice say

140

near him. "Mebbe we can use him if she is. I ain't goin' to kill him till I make shore."

"Yuh're a smart hombre, Red," another man complimented. "It's a good idea. Kinda make her pay a ransom, huh?"

"That's it, Ed," Red Guire agreed. "Mohle told me to sweep up that Circle Three bunch. We need that gal's spread."

It was daylight. Norris could sense that. Despite the blindfold, a bit of light leaked through at one side.

On and on they rode. The sun's hotness told Norris it was the middle of the day, and he was perishing for a drink of water. He sought to make his need known, but no attention was paid him.

He lost consciousness later in the afternoon. The strain was too much for his injured body.

When he again came to, he was lying on the ground, and someone was standing over him.

"Is he dead?"

"Nope, Red. Not yet. But he's nigh to it. Gimme that likker. Water ain't strong enough."

They had been pouring water down his gullet. Now a swig of red-hot whisky was trickled between his parched lips from a tilted bottle.

Norris had no idea where he was. Dazed, he sought to look around. His arms and legs were too weak to move. Over him stood Red Frankie Guire, mask down, sorrel beard bristling from his ugly face. He glowered down at Norris, his crooked, massive legs spread wide. Several other tough-looking hombres, Stetsons carrying the double clip in their Stetsons, masks down in camp, were hanging around. One of them, a bony, black-haired, pock-marked devil, was tending Norris.

"There he comes," Guire growled. He booted Norris with a hard toe. "Behave yoreself, waddy, and yuh won't get hurt no more."

Pete sought to curse, but the words died in his throat. Guire swung on his heels and sauntered off. He sat down and reached for a bottle and a chunk of fried beef.

The stars and moon looked down on the wild scene of the mountain camp. Norris began to regain some strength and realization, lying on the horse blanket that had been spread for him. A guard was over him all the time. They had his hands and ankles tied, but not as tightly as before, so that the circulation wasn't shut off. Dimly he heard the shouts of men.

"Shove 'em down there!"

"Get them fires goin'!"

After Red Guire had finished eating, he lit a quirly and got up.

"C'mon, brand-blotters," he ordered. "That's a big herd and we'll all hafta work tonight. Fetch the prisoner along, Mike."

They hoisted Norris upon a mustang's back, and he was taken along down steep paths, across a little creek. The familiar odor of burnt hair and hide, the sounds of bellowing steers, told him that branding work was going on. He also whiffed a disagreeable, offensive smell that he decided must be burnt wool.

He kept quiet. Trussed up and wounded, he knew he must bide his time and hope that some chance to escape might show later. He hadn't been blindfolded again and he could see some of the scenes that went on.

The stolen steer herd was being driven along in smaller bunches. Evidently they had been split up after the rustlers had made distance to elude pursuit. Norris was astounded at the inside knowledge the thieves showed.

"Mohle," as Guire had named a chief figure, who had ordered the Circle 3 herd stolen, must have been aware of their plans. They believed that Norris liked Sue. Though in his humbleness, Pete hadn't been sure the young woman returned his love, Mohle seemed certain of it.

Chapter XIV
A Waddy Reports

A number of fires were going. Running-irons were being heated in the blazes.

Assistants would rope and throw a cow, hold the beast down. An expert rewrite man, or brand-blotter, would pick up by the handle one of the red-glowing irons, dip a chunk of blanket into a bucket of water. Kneeling over the steer, he would begin to draw the brand into the new design. Like artists, these trained cattle thieves worked, proud of their ability to switch a brand until not even the owner could recognize his former property. The wet blanket, which helped keep the scars from looking too fresh, was wrapped around the end of the iron.

Bellows of pain were torn from the throats of the outraged cattle, but ropes and strong hands held them until the rewrite man was done. Then the beast was loosed and run by waiting horsemen into the finished bunch. Pete Norris watched the eerie scene in the dancing red light of the wood fires. Steep walls hemmed in the creek valley, heavily bushed.

For hours the thieves worked on, rapidly changing brands. It was impossible for Norris to see the marks in the night; for he was some distance away.

There was a gray streak of dawn in the sky when Frankie Guire came waddling up to them.

"Hey, Mike!" called the giant redhead. "Blindfold this young skunk. Yuh better run him on over. I'll be along tomorrer night."

"Okay, Red," replied the dark-skinned Mike.

Again Norris' eyes were covered. For miles he was taken along, in what direction he couldn't guess. For a time they passed through clammy air, the noise of a stream loud in his ears. Finally he was carried inside a building and deposited on a wooden floor.

When his blindfold was off and his cords loosened, he was given food and drink, then left a prisoner in a locked room. He slept for some hours.

Waking, he felt refreshed and stronger. The walls about him were revealed in the light from a small window, across which bars had been nailed outside. They looked too strong to break.

He managed to free his hands by rubbing the loose bonds on the edge of the bunk, then got his feet untied. But the door, when he tried it, was locked.

Again night had fallen, by the time he awoke. Voices came to him from another room. The partitions were thick boards, but there were cracks between.

"I got new orders," a man said. "We're gonna clean up Warwick and use this entire county. Get every fightin' man together that you can, Red, and mass 'em for attack. Mohle's tired of the opposition and he aims to wipe it out. They got six of our boys in Warwick jail, because of that Jim Harris sidewinder. We gotta get 'em out. Then this stockmen's patrol in Warwick is a damned nuisance. Jest kill everyone you spot. I'll furnish yuh with fifty fightin' men."

"Good," growled Red Frankie Guire. "It suits me fine. I'll muster a hundred and fifty guns ag'in 'em. Tell Mohle I'll be ready in forty-eight hours."

Pete Norris' blood ran cold as he heard the horrible plan of destruction being plotted in the other room.

"I gotta get outa here, somehow," he vowed with grim desperation.

It had been a tight squeeze for the tall

Ranger and the patrol, up in the trap-gulch of the western hills. But his power and fighting ability had turned the tide. When the smoke of the terrific battle cleared, Hatfield had emerged victorious. They had lost five men in death, and eight had been wounded. Even Durban and his deputy Ben Walton, and others who had been in back when the trap shut, had minor wounds and scratches.

In the conflict Hatfield had captured six of the rustlers, hard-faced devils who cursed him furiously as he lined them up. They had lit that fire as a draw, to bring the patrol into the gulch. But they refused to give him any information. Cocky, sure of their gang's strength and ability to rescue them, they had buttoned their lips. Tough-hided, nasty-eyed, the cattle thieves defied the law.

Sheriff Durban, self-important over the capture, insisted on taking charge of the captives.

"No lynchin', gents," he stated. "The law'll take its rightful course."

The Texas Rangers didn't believe in lynching, either. Hatfield was willing enough that the prisoners be taken back to stand trial. But Tad Durban disliked the tall waddy, couldn't seem to swallow his first suspicions of Hatfield. He refused to let anyone but himself take charge of the rustlers.

147

They were mounted on spare mustangs, hands tied to saddle-horns. The work of burying the dead had been finished. Leaving behind them the stone-covered mounds of friends and foes, the patrol started back for Warwick.

Hatfield was the first man to hit the main street. The first person to greet him was Sue Atchinson, who came hurrying across the plaza to look up at him. The eager life was gone from her pretty eyes, and her face was pale.

"Oh, Jim, I'm glad you're back!" she cried in distraction.

"What's wrong, Miss Sue?" he asked gently as he dismounted.

"They got our herd, Jim. And — Pete Norris must have been killed. He hasn't come back or been seen at all."

Hot fury streaked through Hatfield's heart. It was all he could do to maintain control of his features. The girl, bravely holding back her tears, told him the news.

Two thousand head of prime steers had been rustled from the U No, south of Warwick. Three range riders had been slaughtered by the thieves, after being run north while the patrol was on the long chase to the west. The rustlers had scooped up the Circle 3 bunch and split up and disappeared

148

in the dense brush. Only two of the Circle 3 waddies had come limping back to Warwick with the sad story. Both were wounded, and had escaped by the skin of their teeth from Red Guire's big main band of cattle thieves.

"They drawed us off, I reckon," muttered Hatfield, "so's to pull off that U No job and sweep up the little herd that was supposed to save the Circle Three."

"Do you think they killed Pete?" she asked anxiously.

Plainly she was far more disturbed over the possible fate of Norris than about her ranch.

"Take it easy, ma'am," Hatfield told her softly. "I'll find him." To himself he added the reservation: "Dead or alive."

He didn't have much hope that the rustlers would have spared Norris. However, he didn't want to smash Sue's hopes.

"Billy Frisch was one of the two boys who got away, wounded," she continued. "He said he found Pete's white mare, Betsy, shot to death but not trampled. But there's no sign of Pete's body at all."

"Where's Frisch now?" asked the Ranger. "I'd like to talk to him."

"He's lying up in a room at the Drovers Cottage," she replied.

Hatfield nodded, left her. He paused to

toss down a drink at the New York and then ambled over to the Drovers Cottage, which served as a hotel in Warwick. He found Frisch, a young fellow in his early twenties, a big, tow-headed Texan with light-blue eyes and a good strong jaw. Billy had worked faithfully for Hatfield at the Circle 3 and knew the country. He had taken a rustler bullet through the shoulder, and another had cut a nasty gash in his bronzed, smooth cheek.

"How yuh feelin', Billy?"

"Okay," Frisch replied, searching the tall man's gray-green eyes.

"Yuh lost Norris and three men and the herd, huh?"

"Yeah." Frisch dropped his glance. Though it hadn't been his fault, he felt ashamed at having been bested. "They over-run us, Jim. Couple thousand steers and mebbe forty gunnies."

"Reckon they knowed yuh was there?"

Frisch swore explosively.

"I'm shore of it!"

"Huh," Hatfield breathed. "Mighty handy for Vane, seein' he wants the Circle Three. But why's he after it? I'm shore goin' to find out. A trip to the Star Eight comes next in line."

"Harry was too bad hit to ride far,"

continued Frisch. "But I tried to trail 'em when I got my breath and was able to keep on my hoss. They went straight north full-speed for some hours, till they come to the thick chaparral of the foothills. Then they split into a couple dozen bunches and went off in all directions. I lost the sign I was on. You savvy there's millions of hoofprints on that range, criss-crossin' every which way. The land bein' so dry and hard, it don't hold prints much."

"I savvy. Yuh got any guess which way they took?"

"Well, it wouldn't be south. We was that-away, and so's Warwick and flatter country. The east is blocked complete by the Comanches. Nothin' but a mountain sheep could cross 'em. And you and yore patrol was to the west, and yuh woulda spotted 'em as yuh returned. North is the only way left. I figger these rustler devils split up and then met some miles further up, at a spot they agreed on. When they get outa the district, they head for the Pecos, cross way up north, drivin' slower and easier, not needin' so many men. That country up there is plumb deserted. They could hop over into New Mexico, where she snugs into the Panhandle, then finally make Kansas and ship from there."

"Yuh may be right, 'cause it all fits," agreed Hatfield. "Do you s'pose they've killed Norris?"

Frisch shrugged, grimaced in pain. Without meaning to, he had moved his stiff, wounded shoulder.

"Dunno why they'd save him, Jim," he admitted. "Still, we didn't find his body."

"Mighta been trampled right into the ground in that stampede," suggested Hatfield.

"Yeah. He mighta been shot off before they got Betsy, who run clear. Still, we didn't even find a shred of his clothes. We didn't find nothin'."

After finishing his chat with the wounded Frisch, the tall Ranger strolled over to the jail. Ben Walton stood on guard outside. A knot of angry, muttering cowmen had gathered nearby and were casting red-eyed, furious looks at the adobe walls of the lockup. Lynch talk was being bandied about.

Jim Hatfield went to the door. Walton grinned at him.

"Howdy, big feller. Yuh want in?"

"Yeah. Ask the sheriff to let me have a word with them cattle thieves."

Walton knocked three times. The door was unbolted and Tad Durban poked his head out.

"What yuh want?" he demanded.

"How about lettin' me question them rustlers, Sheriff?" drawled the Ranger. "Pete Norris ain't been found, either dead or alive. Mebbe them sidewinders can help clear up a lot of our trouble."

Durban frowned. "I'll tend to 'em, Harris. Any questioning to be done, I'll do it my ownself. I'm protectin' my prisoners, with guns if I hafta. I don't need no more deputies to do no detective work. I reckon I can do that without no help."

Hatfield stared into the black, close-set eyes. The loutish sheriff was no friend of his, for Durban evidently couldn't shake off his original suspicion of the tall hombre. The burly sheriff was bristling at him now, obviously intending to snatch the glory of the arrest for himself. A big iron key-ring hung at Durban's wide black-leather belt, which held up his six-shooters. He was truculent, quick to defend his dignity.

"Okay, Sheriff," drawled the Ranger, swinging away.

He wasn't ready to call the turn. The prisoners would not be likely to break down yet, since they probably expected rescue and protection from their powerful gang. Only cruel and extraordinary measures that the sheriff wouldn't allow and Rangers disliked using might have got anything out of them.

CHAPTER XV
THE LAME COW

It was late in the afternoon. The evening express rumbled in the distance, and its black smoke trail refused to dissipate in the hot blue sky. Its roar rapidly increased in volume as it came tearing through Warwick at top speed, tooting at the crossings, swirling rubble and dust in its furious wake.

Goldy had to rest and needed a feed. So did the battered Ranger, who had been in saddle for a couple of days with but snatches of sleep. When the end of the day was near, he found a bed in a haymow of the stable where the sorrel was being fed.

A wrangler awoke him early in the morning.

"Lady askin' for yuh, Boss."

Hatfield rose, pulled his boots on. The rest had refreshed him. It was a windy morning, with dust puffing in spurts across the scrofulous plaza. Warwick seemed quiet in the coolness of the dawn.

The Ranger went out front and greeted Sue Atchinson. Her face was anxious. She bit her lip as she looked at his grave, strong face.

"Somethin's shore hit her, she's so excited and scaired," he decided. Aloud he asked: "What is it, ma'am?"

She couldn't meet his gaze for long.

"Jim, I've decided to quit. I simply can't hold out at the Circle Three any longer, so I'm going to sell. You've been mighty fine and I wanted to thank you for trying."

"We ain't quittin' yet," he replied.

"I am." She was curiously firm, almost hysterical about it. "I tell you, I'm going to sell."

"To Vane's Star Eight Syndicate?"

"No. I haven't heard from them again. But I — I'm going to sell."

He tried to make her meet his eyes. She could not.

"Well, then," he drawled, "I reckon I'll go hunt for Pete Norris."

"Please don't. Just forget it, Jim. Forget everything."

"Now look," he told her gently, "I tried to help yuh, Miss Sue. What're yuh hidin' from me?"

"Nothing."

She stared right into his eyes. Women, he thought, could be mighty stubborn at times, even if they did seem soft. She was lying brazenly. He was aware how she felt about Norris and she had been anxious to hunt for him the day before. Then he guessed the reason. It was perfectly logical.

"Ransom," he growled. "That's it. If yuh sell the Circle Three, Norris comes back. I'll get a posse and scour the country!"

"You — you —" she gasped. Tears sprang to her pretty eyes and a white line of terror tighted about her coral lips. "Jim, you must be careful. They'll — they'll kill Pete if you tell the sheriff or try to get up a posse."

"Then yuh've heard from 'em and Norris ain't dead."

She seized his muscular forearm in pleading entreaty.

"Let me settle it, Jim. I'll gladly give them the ranch if they'll free Pete."

"What makes yuh think they'll let him go, once they've won? He'd make a mighty dangerous witness against 'em. Who is it? Vane?"

His shrewd deductions had exposed what she wished to hide. She was trying now only to convince him.

"No, it's not Vane. It's true that I haven't heard from him again! A stranger, a man I never saw before, came to me early today. He hinted that if I'd let him have the Circle Three at his price, Pete would be freed.

156

Then he rode off, northwest. I don't dare delay. He said someone else would be back tomorrow to take the deed to the ranch. But if I breathed a word to the law or anyone else, they'd know about it and I'd never again see Pete."

"Mighty bold devils," mused the tall Ranger, turning the information over in his quick, clever brain.

"You promise me you won't interfere?"

"I'd shore hate to lose Norris," he evaded.

She took it that he was agreeing with her. She stood on tiptoe, smiling in relief, and kissed him lightly on the cheek. Then she turned and hurried across the plaza, toward the house where she was staying.

For a moment he stared after her. Then he shrugged, went over to Walton's Chow House. The waitress smiled dazedly at him and sought to draw his attention by waiting on him with an extra flourish. However, while he stowed away a hearty meal, he was preoccupied with his thoughts.

"Must be Vane," he decided. "They've got their nerve with 'em, forcin' the issue." Vague uneasiness seized upon him, for he figured the hidden, powerful foes he was bucking must be quite sure of themselves to try such a game. "They'll hafta kill me and a lot of others, before they'll be safe in these parts."

What he had learned cinched it. He must take a run over to the Star 8 and check up there.

"Mohle," he muttered, out on the walk. "I'll wire McDowell."

A visit to the telegraph office took ten minutes. Then he saddled up the golden sorrel, which had been rested and fed.

Brant Tazewell and a bunch of cowmen were on the plaza, near the jail. He rode over toward them.

"Where yuh bound, Jim?" called out Tazewell.

"I'm gonna ride to the U No and see about that big bunch they lost. Be back tomorrer."

"Okay. Take care of yoreself."

He raised a hand, sang out "Adios." He rode across the tracks and headed south. He kept going for several miles, until the gently rising contours hid him from Warwick. Then he turned east, rode at a swift pace under the cloud-filled sky. Wind blew the dust into great swirls, as the fast hoofs of the sorrel cut it up, and rattled the dry pods of the mesquite.

When he figured he was far enough along, he cut north and crossed the railroad onto the Star 8 main range. But he kept to the west of the ranch spur, where he had run into trouble that first day in the vicinity.

"I ain't got much to go on," he muttered aloud to the gelding. "Nothin' but guesses ag'in Vane."

The southern spurs of the Comanches towered not far to his left, rising into steep, impassable red and gray cliffs that were covered with scrub pine and chaparral. There were bunches of steers about. But to the south, the range here was too sandy to support many cows.

"Main range must be north," he decided, keeping along the irregular line of the rising mountains.

As he rode mile after mile, though, with the wind flinging gritty alkali particles into his face, he saw no first-class cow lands.

At noon he paused for a time to rest the sorrel. He drank from canteen and munched cold food stored in his saddlebags. Then he went on. He couldn't approach the Star 8 buildings closely in the daytime, for there were too many hands around the big spread.

Several steers galloped off from his line of approach, tails up. They drew only a glance from the alert gray-green eyes. He had seen hundreds of them, Star 8 brand on their rumps. They all looked alike, for one steer was just the same as another.

The high Comanches cast a long shadow over the rolling prairie land, cut up by mesquite and chaparral. In this he rode for hour after hour. Bands of cows kept moving off from his vicinity.

"Yeah, they're as like as peas in a pod," he muttered. "Mighty hard to identify stolen cattle." But suddenly an electric shock went through him. "No, they ain't! C'mon, Goldy. Let's rope that critter!"

Among the latest bunch of steers he had raised, he spotted the strange cow which had so amused him during the little roundup he had staged at the Circle 3. There she was, left hind leg bent out, running with her scuttling, comical gait. The big white splashes on her sides were clearly visible.

The swift sorrel's hoofs drummed rapidly as Goldy guessed what his master was after. Pointed toward the strange cow, the sorrel quickly realized that it was this animal Hatfield wanted to lasso, and kept after her. As they drew closer, the others scattering to the sides, the battered cow looked around. The Ranger noted the scar where the lost horn had been torn out.

"No doubt at all," he mused. "Now how did she get through here?"

The lariat whistled through the air, settled over the splotched cow's head. The sorrel slid to a stop, feet braced, and the saddle-horn took the shock. The cow was yanked around and fell heavily on her side, bawling in complaint.

"Hold her, Goldy!"

The gelding pulled back his head, keeping the line taut so his master could hustle along it and hogtie the steer.

As an expert, Hatfield was intensely inter-ested in the brand. It was a Star 8. The scab was still on, the hair about it singed, not yet covering the owner's mark. He felt it over with his fingers as the cow shivered and protested. Strands of some foreign sub-stance clung to the burned hide.

"Wool," he decided, "from a blanket-covered iron. It's a good job of switchin'. Best I ever saw."

This animal had been in the Circle 3 bunch that was stolen from Pete Norris on the route to Warwick. It was impossible for her to have wandered around the southern toes of the Comanches in such a short time, even if she had escaped the herd and not been spotted by Frisch and Harry.

"The old game," he muttered. "Settin' up a brand close to one that can be run over easy."

The Star was made by thickening the circumference of the circle as it was blotted out into points. Changing a "3" to an "8" was a cinch for a good rewrite man.

Goldy shifted behind him. He released the trussed steer. As she scuttled off, kicking out her bent leg, he stood staring at the dark wall of the wooded, steep Comanches.

The sorrel brought him back to his danger, sniffing beside his ear as he gazed toward the mountains.

"Yuh're right, Goldy. This is no place to be day-dreamin'."

He mounted. From saddle-height he saw some dust toward the buildings of the big Syndicate's headquarters.

"Thanks for the warnin'," he said. He spurred west, toward a thick clump of high mesquite that was alive with starry white blooms. Hidden in the brush, he waited, peering out.

Holding the quiet sorrel's reins, he observed a big band of riders headed west for the mountains. He was glad he hadn't skinned the cow he had roped. They would have run upon him as he worked. Goldy's keen equine senses had saved him the danger of exposure.

The horsemen came within a quarter-mile of his hiding place. Straining his sharp eyes, he recognized several of them as Star 8 waddies. Some of them had tried to stop him on his way over, when he had killed a steer for meat.

"Didn't think I was a rustler. They figgered I was a range detective skinnin' a critter to check the brand."

They passed his line and kept going west, into the swiftly rising hills. Two great mountain peaks towered against one another, dark slopes broken here and there by needle spires of red rock.

"They shore look impassable," he mused, "but they ain't. That's a cinch."

The presence of the strange-looking cow had given him the clue he needed. There were a few more hours of daylight left. He didn't dare ride on the direct trail of the fifty Star 8 punchers he'd spotted, for he didn't wish to lose his advantage.

He was able to make some westing by using the thickening clumps of mesquite. Then he hit an arroyo, a dry ditch running approximately the way he wished to go, and rode along it.

CHAPTER XVI
THE PASS

Resting till dark fell suddenly over the wilds, Hatfield made straight for the spot in the chaparral where he had last seen the Star 8 riders. He had taken his bearings from the looming black mountain peaks, framed against the glimpsed stars. The moon glowed bright and then low, behind running clouds. He could hear the wind shrieking overhead in the cliffs, rustling the dry chaparral.

The bush was like a blank wall, but he was not fooled. Dismounting, he found a pass through high rocks and trees. Hidden from view, even up close, the cunningly screened trail wound west through a narrow cut. It was slow going in the darkness. He had to use his keen sense of touch, smell and hearing.

What kept drawing him was the sound of distant running water. He left the sorrel behind in a dense thicket. Crawling close, he saw the sudden red glow of a cigarette as a man sitting on a rock under a beetling cliff drew deeply on his quirly.

Hatfield froze, seeking to orient himself. The shadows were black as pitch. After a few minutes, as he inched toward the casually puffing sentinel, he heard the *clop-clop* of horse's hoofs on stone, then a voice, startling loud as it echoed in the high walls of rock.

"Okay, Steve. I'll take it. You can go on to camp."

A man had suddenly ridden right out of the red rock cliff, was taking over the guard position.

"They gettin' ready?" asked Steve, preparing to mount and leave.

"Yeah, shinin' guns and fillin' up on bullets. I hate to miss it, but I got a nasty wound in the side from that big jigger when we hit him at the Circle Three."

"*Adios,* then."

"*Adios.*"

Hatfield had taken advantage of their voices to cover his advance. He could see the dark shape of the horseman, Steve, riding on his way. The hombre who had come to take Steve's place was looking after him. The sound of the running water was loud, helping to cover the slight sounds Hatfield's boots made as he moved, crouched over.

Hogleg out, he struck unerringly with the barrel, laying it with a dull crack on the guard's temple. The hombre folded up like a jumping-jack with a broken string. The

165

Ranger caught him by the throat, but it wasn't necessary to cut off his cries. The blow from the Colt barrel had knocked him out.

Swiftly the Ranger gagged and bound him, carried him over to a clump of bush and laid him out. He figured it would be hours before they sent another sentry to relieve this one and found him missing. They didn't appear to be worried over the possibility that this side of the secret pass might be discovered. No doubt they felt quite safe with the Star 8 on that side.

"Now I savvy why they wanted Sue Atchinson's," he thought as he prepared to trail Steve.

There was a gate in the cliff, around a perpendicular shelf. Water splashed about his knees as he slipped and nearly went down, off the path. Listening, he could hear the hollow, echoing sound of the horse's hoofs ahead of him.

It was like a tunnel. The little stream plunged into a hole as it emerged from the mountain base and disappeared. Eventually it came up miles eastward as springs and waterholes for the Star 8.

There was a path, well trodden by many hoofs, sticky clay alongside the winding cut made by the creek. On and on, trailing the rider up front, the Ranger hurried. It was black as ink in the tunnel and he had to feel a way with his hands. The sound of the water was loud, enough to drown out the noises he made when he slipped occasionally.

The tunnel, which cut between the two giant Comanche peaks, was nearly a half-mile through. It twisted this way and that, but it was big enough for a horse to go through.

"And a steer," Hatfield added.

Having discovered the important secret of the great rustler band, he eagerly shoved on. At last he saw a rectangular spot of night sky ahead. The reddish glow, he figured, must be from a fire. In its light was framed the sentry, Steve, who had unwittingly led him through the rustler pass.

Hatfield came out where the creek disappeared into dense chaparral. The trail swung right around the toes of the big western peak. He knew he was on the western side of the Comanches, save for minor hills interposing between his position and the Circle 3 range. Crouched in the shadows, he stared out across the narrow valley made by the stream. The fire was burning up to the left, south of him. Steve was making for it.

The Ranger crept on toward a higher point. He was aware as he drew closer of a growling hum of masculine voices. From a safe distance he looked down upon the rustlers' camp.

"Must be a hundred and twenty, mebbe more," he thought.

The vast array of gunnies was grouped round the central fire, shaded in the shallow, flattened-out, basinlike depression. The smell of fried food and the sheen of the fire on bottles revealed that they were stoking up. He noted that many of them were busy shining their rifles and pistols. Boxes of ammunition, their lids broken open, stood where the fighters could help themselves.

Steve turned his horse into a corral made of rough limbs below the main rustler stronghold, which was well guarded on the west. He went up to join his partners. A giant hombre stepped to the center. Hatfield recognized Red Frankie Guire, leader of the cattle thieves when they went on their terrible, far-reaching raids over Texas.

"Get loaded up good, boys," he ordered. "We start at dawn, ride to within strikin' distance. Then we'll hide, rest and be ready to hit after dark the next night."

A rumble of satisfaction rose in the bearded rustlers' throats, along with boasts of what each gunny would do in battle. Hat-field couldn't get in any closer.

"Now where they mean to hit?" he wondered. "Mebbe another big ranch, like the U No."

Every moment was fraught with the danger of discovery. He had no horse, and if the gang chanced to spot him, he would be torn to pieces by their bullets. Guns bristled everywhere. He knew too well how much they would enjoy seeing his blood stain the ground. He was blocked from rounding the camp. Besides, he glimpsed a couple of alert sentries up on the rim to the east.

"That's the one way they look for trouble," he decided.

Shrewdly he was already calculating the chance of catching the gang in their secret camp. By the time the guard he had laid out on the other side of the tunnel came to, though, they would be on their way to some fresh atrocity.

"Hafta get back and round the south spurs," he determined. "If I could get in here with enough fightin' men, I might grab the camp and catch them rustlers unsuspectin', when they rode home tired out."

There was nothing more to be gained by staying around there. He carefully began to retreat, reached the secret tunnel pass and returned the way he had come. Goldy nuzzled him slightly.

He mounted, swung the gelding east toward the Star 8 ranch. Looking the spread over was too good a chance to be passed up, for the bulk of its riders had ridden to join Red Guire's gang.

Around midnight he saw the lights of the big house ahead. If he could, he meant to go in.

The Ranger sneaked afoot toward the great, rambling house of the Star 8. He had removed his spurs and chaps so that he could move with more facility and quiet. They hung from the saddle of the golden sorrel, which he had hidden out in the high mesquite.

It was late, but there was a lamp burning in the large front room. The place appeared quiet. The long bunkhouse, where usually slept the minions of George Vane, was dark, its door shut. However, as Hatfield crouched, peering through the gnarled branches of ratama that grew along the bar fence encircling the buildings, he saw a man walk from the rear of the house and go into one of the sheds.

Circling around, he plotted his course, approaching from the shadowed side. The scudding black clouds helped to conceal him as he reached a side window that looked into the main room. He peeked over the sill.

George Vane was sitting in a chair at the round table, smoking and reading a newspaper. The manager's black patent-leather hair gleamed in the yellow lamplight. He wore neat, clean clothing. His head was bent as he read.

Hatfield had been here in the daytime, and knew the general layout of the spread. To the east, some hundreds of yards away, were the great cattle pens along the railway spur, with loading chute. The Star 8 had its own shipping facilities. At specified times, cattle cars were shunted in. The office was a square wing built on the side. Now it was dark, the outside door closed and bolted inside.

A wraith in the night, Hatfield approached. One of the windows gave to the upward pressure of his knife blade, and he slowly inched up the sash. Once it gave a sharp creak. He froze, listened for whole minutes before proceeding. He cautiously slipped inside and stood there, waiting for his eyes to accustom themselves to the darkness.

Eventually he could make out a large, flat-topped desk, a green-painted safe with "Star

8" on its door and some chairs. On a shelf stood two big ledgers. These were what he was after. Every ranch had to keep books, even as crooked a one as he was now convinced the Star 8 was. Cattle associations required records, and Vane's Syndicate was supposedly honest. At any time an inspector might ride up and demand access to the books, and these must check with railroad way-bills of heads shipped.

In the vague shaft of light from the windows, he lifted down the heavy ledgers, laid them on the floor beside the green safe. He took off his wide-brimmed Stetson and used it as a shield under which to strike a match so he could read the figures in the accounting books.

March . . . . . 3,987 head
April . . . . . 2,345 head

"Whew!" he muttered. "That range'd never support anything like it!"

With the other proof he had been collecting, he figured he could wreck the Star 8. He struck several matches, blocking off the tiny flares with his crouched body, his head bent low. The corner in which stood the safe also helped to hide the tiny flames.

Suddenly the door which led into the

main house was flung back. The accusing, straight beam of a bull's-eye lantern struck his curved back, showed up his crouched figure over the ledgers.

"You don't need to check up on me," an amused voice said. "I'm on the square."

Hatfield spun around on his toes, reaching swiftly for his six-shooter. The thick steel safe was ample protection against bullets. He slipped back of it.

The hombre who had sneaked in on him was George Vane, manager of the Star 8. Evidently he had heard some slight sound, perhaps the creak of the raising window, and had come to the office. At first he had believed that a suspicious associate was looking over the books in an effort to catch him cheating. But the lantern showed who it really was.

"Blast you, Harris!" roared Vane.

"Throw up yore hands and keep shut," ordered the Ranger, Colt rising, hammer-spur back under his thumb.

There was a crash as Vane dropped the lantern and leaped back into the hall. An instant later the manager's pistol spurted flame. Lead spattered above the crouched Ranger as bullets smashed against the heavy metal of the safe.

Hatfield let go once, but Vane was quick

on his feet. Hatfield knew he had not hit him right, for he could hear the boss of the Star 8 shouting.

"Boys, this way! Block the offices. There's a thief in there. Hustle and rouse him out!"

The lantern hadn't been extinguished by the fall. The flame caught the spilled oil and began rising, licking along the dry wood of the floor close to the half-open door.

Jim Hatfield leaped to his feet, six-shooter up and covering the door. Vane was yelling, and answering cries came from all around.

The Ranger started for the open window. A bullet shrieked at an angle through the door crack and thudded within inches of him in the wall. He turned to shoot back, hold Vane down. Then another slug spat through the glass of the upper window, making a round hole in it and cutting just above his black hair.

Colts blasting, he drove back to the other side. He struck at the glass with his gun barrel. About to leap outside, he heard a cry from inside the house.

"Circle Three, this way! Circle Three, this way!"

"It's Pete Norris!" Hatfield gasped.

Chapter XVII
Battle at the Star

The burning oil, smoke coming up with the fire, was spreading and threatening to get a real start. Hatfield couldn't leave Norris there, to be killed in the flames. Pete must be tied, probably locked in.

The Ranger pivoted, dashed full-tilt for the hall. The flames licked at his leather-clad legs as he passed through. Acrid smoke blinded his eyes and caught at his throat. Then he was through, traveling fast.

Vane was down the hall, with a couple of his fighting men. The ranch guards left behind, running past him to engage and cut off the Ranger. One had a double-barreled, sawed-off shotgun in his hands. As Hatfield emerged from the smoke, he threw it up. Buckshot could be deadly, even though not accurately aimed.

Hatfield knew it only too well. His Colt snapped an instant ahead of the shotgun. The killer was falling forward, even as his fingers squeezed the first trigger. The full load drove into the floor as the gunny died on the spot.

Vane's fancy pistol blared. Hatfield felt the sting of the lead as it creased his chest and shrieked on down the hall. The reply

175

from the Ranger's hogleg drilled a chunk of flesh from the second gunny's thigh, half-whirling him around and ruining his aim. The Ranger bullet, after passing through the gunman, evidently skewered Vane. The manager dropped one arm. With a screech of pain, he fell, rolling back into the main room.

"Circle Three, this way! Help, Circle Three!"

Pete Norris was yelling from the rear of the big house. Hatfield, watching back over his shoulder, ran past the office door and through the smoke, heading for the sound.

"Norris, keep yellin'!" he shouted.

"This way, Circle Three!" Pete obliged.

The Ranger burst out into the dining room, a great, square chamber at the middle of the house. A man with a pistol in hand was just running from the door on the other side.

"Throw it down!" ordered Hatfield tersely.

The hombre's eyes grew scared as he saw the tall, rugged Ranger charging his way. He blinked, turned and raced back along the hall, shouting for help. Hatfield reloaded his Colt as he ran. He had another in a holster at his other side.

"Circle Three, here I am! Get me out!"

The barred door was between the kitchen

lean-to and the dining room. Besides being bolted with two iron bars, it had a padlock and chain. The bolts were easily drawn. Hatfield stuck his gun against the padlock and let go. The bullet blew it wide open. He unhooked the chain from the loop, kicked in the door.

"Jim!"

Pete Norris, though pale and weak, was alive and still able to grin at him.

"Where's yore friends?" Norris asked.

"I'm alone."

"Doggone!" exclaimed Pete.

He caught the Colt the Ranger tossed him. Hatfield, his spare hogleg in his long, slim hand, peered out to see if the coast were clear. Vane was yelling up front.

"Stop him! Get him! Shoot the dog!"

Heavy footfalls shook the house. Confusion had seized upon the ranch.

"Foller me," ordered the tall Ranger.

He jumped out into the corridor, gun blasting. A trio of hard-eyed devils blocking the exit to the rear fell over themselves to escape the driving lead. There was an open door down the way. Hatfield could see the window beyond, and shoved Norris inside.

"We'll take the winder, Pete. Keep with me now. Got to pick up a horse for yuh."

Shrilly he whistled to bring in the golden

177

sorrel. Goldy was waiting for him out in the mesquite.

"There they go, round to the side!"

"Fire!" someone else was yelling. "Fetch some buckets!"

Fury against the tall man who had dared enter the Star 8 alone, who had downed several of them and nicked their boss Vane, was mounting high. The home guard was rapidly pulling itself together, converging from bunkhouse, stables and the cook's quarters.

Hatfield knew they had but a minute or two in which to make good their escape, before the first shock of his bullets wore off and they were overwhelmed. Already he heard men running from both directions along the hall toward the room. He poked his head and shoulders out of the window, glimpsed a couple of them rounding the front of the house to cut him off.

"Here we go," he told Norris.

He dived out, landing on his shoulder and rolling into fighting position. A couple of slugs whipped past him, too close for comfort as he moved. He took aim, that cool instant which means the difference between hit or miss. When he fired, one of the gunnies staggered against his mate.

Norris came out, hit the dry ground at his

178

side. With Pete in the scrap, the Star 8 hombre had to jump back to the veranda rail, hunting cover.

The two men ran for the shadows of the yard. Cries and gunshots rang about them. George Vane sought to whip his fighters into order, but he hadn't more than eighteen or twenty at the ranch. Most of them were out with Red Guire.

Hatfield's breath rasped in and out of his deep, powerful lungs. He was bleeding from nicks taken in the scrap. Pounding hoofs drew them south. Vane, urging on a dozen gunnies, whirled around the front. As shotguns and pistols were seeking the escaping pair, Goldy came galloping up.

"Get aboard," ordered the tall Ranger, peering back over his haunched shoulder. "He can carry double a ways."

Norris obeyed. The Ranger jumped up behind him. They sprinted behind the stable toward one of the horse corrals, in which bunched a number of mustangs.

"There they are," roared Vane. "After 'em, boys!"

A volley missed the moving sorrel and his double load. Hatfield kicked at the corral gate. Norris leaped down, got hold of a dark-hided mustang's bridle and mounted bareback. The futile lead of the Star 8 angrily buzzed about their lowered heads as they rode hell-for-leather toward the south.

Panting, they kept going, content just to make distance. Some of the gunmen rode out in pursuit, but it was ineffective. The two out front had a good start and the night was dark, the rolling range studded with protective patches of mesquite and giant cactus growths.

A couple of miles south of the spread, the Ranger slowed, and Norris came up beside him.

"So they didn't kill yuh," Hatfield growled.

"Nope. Blast 'em, it was Red Guire who took me, Jim. They got our herd, run over us in the night. I feel mighty bad at losin' Sue's ranch for her."

"It ain't gone yet. She aims to sell it, though, to ransom yuh."

"Where the devil are we, anyway? What spread is that?"

"It's the Star Eight, Vane's outfit."

"Star Eight? I musta been asleep a long while, if they toted me all the way around the mountains!"

Hatfield figured, however, that Norris had been taken through the secret pass used by the rustlers. They swung their horses' noses for Warwick, many hours' ride west and south.

"Jim," Pete said, "I overheard some terrible plans Red Guire aims to carry out. He mentioned some hombre named Mohle, who seems to be the boss of the lot. They mean to hit Warwick with a hundred and fifty fightin' men, kill the ranchers in the county who oppose 'em, and rescue some of their friends Durban's got in jail. And they shore got it in for yuh. They'll skin yuh alive if they ever take yuh."

Behind them the new day was rising, streaking the eastern sky with pale light. Stars still showed in the heavens above and ahead of them, over the mountains. Norris was worn to a frazzle, weak from the ordeal he had undergone, still suffering from his wounds.

They stopped after sunrise, when they sighted a muddy waterhole around which some Star 8 cows were standing. As the riders came up, the steers galloped off from over the rise. They dismounted, to wash and drink. Goldy's handsome hide was covered with splashes of mud, the lather dried to a crust.

"Someone comin'," warned Pete.

The lean young trail boss had washed and was drying himself with what was left of his shirt. Hatfield lay on his belly, bathing his nicked scalp and bronzed face in the water. The Ranger rose, buckling on his gun-belt.

"It's Vane," he growled.

The chief of the Star 8, astride a big blue mustang, was spurring toward Warwick. He had a dozen armed waddies as an escort and had got west of them, evidently without knowing their position. He didn't appear to be hunting them. Now he had them cut off from the direct route to town. The water-hole was in a shallow, wide depression. Considerable bush was around, but not enough to screen them entirely.

Vane, spurring his blue around the rim a mile away, suddenly spotted them. He whirled his mustang and pointed. His men quickly unshipped their rifles.

Hatfield grabbed his Winchester from its saddle-sling, for long-range guns had to be dealt with in kind. A revolver would be totally ineffective.

"C'mon, Pete!" he ordered. "Get mounted!"

He hit leather as Vane spread his men out and started for them. A bullet kicked up a spurt of dust to the right.

Hatfield brought the Winchester to his shoulder, took aim. It was a good distance, but they were moving rather slowly, intent on the enemy in the rising sunlight. Neither side wished to come to close grips.

After running along with them for a couple of miles, George Vane dropped off. He turned his blue stallion and rode southwest toward Warwick, while his men kept on after the slowly retiring pair. The Star 8 riders were holding a strung-out line between the Ranger and the direct route to town.

An hour of this cat-and-mouse game, exchanging rifle bullets at long range, and the Ranger knew he wasn't getting where he wanted to go.

"I'll hafta get through, even if it means shootin' eye to eye," he growled to Norris. "Vane'll beat me to Warwick. I'd sorta hoped he'd head the other way, not to town. It'll be dark before I can make it now."

His idea had been that Vane, wishing to report to a superior on the Ranger's spying at the Star 8, would make for the tunnel pass through the Comanches. But Vane was clearly on his way to Warwick.

Even at this morning hour, it was already so hot that they felt like baked potatoes in their leather as they rode through low scrub chaparral. Long-thorned bushes covered the rolling land, interspersed by cactus flats. Every plant in the Big Bend could stick, sting or had a bad odor. Hatfield and Norris, knowing the species of growths, avoided a clump of "It Blinds the Goat," which had fine spines that flew off when an animal came too close.

Lying on patches of bare ground were old "leather-buttons," really peyote plants from which Indians distilled a narcotic drink. Creosote and ratama, prickly pear, bayonet, giant cactus thrusting thirty and forty feet up with candelabra arms, barrel cactus, mesquite and the ocotillo all flourished in Brewster.

Hatfield looked back. When they slowed down, the Star 8 gained ground. The rifle bullets plugged too near for comfort, or shrieked in the hot air about their heads. A lucky hit would mean the end. There was no suitable cover. Whatever rocks they saw were ledge outcroppings or too small for use.

The Ranger stared south. The land shimmered, flat and useless, mile after mile toward the Mexican border. Goldy had had a long run and it was a day's ride to Warwick. The sorrel needed all the reserves he packed in his magnificent muscles.

Scintillatingly the sun flashed on long lines of steel — the railroad, running east and west. As he sighted the tracks in the eastern distance, Hatfield's keen ears caught the rumble of a train.

"C'mon, Pete," he ordered. "I got an idea."

Chapter XVIII
The Race to Town

They slanted for the tracks. A plume of black coal smoke was coming toward them. As the long freight approached, going at a slow rate of speed, Hatfield waited till the puffing steam engine was almost abreast of them.

Abruptly he spurred Goldy across to the other side. Norris was right with him. The engine man leaned from his cab, cursing them and shaking his fist.

The rumbling grind of the wheels and the creak of box cars drowned out the shouts of the Star 8 gang. All but one had been caught on the north side as the Ranger and Norris rode alongside a red car, protected by the wheel trucks and sides.

The Star 8 rider, upon whom they quickly came, stared with sudden alarm as he realized that he was alone. He fired a couple of shots that harmlessly splintered the wooden flank of the box car, then spurred hell-for-leather out of the way of the

Ranger's crashing rifle. The hombre's horse suddenly stumbled and the rider flew head over heels into a clump of prickly pear. They heard his shrieks dimly as they passed, easily keeping abreast of the chugging train.

The rest of the gunnies, heading back for the caboose, came around the train finally. But the Ranger and Norris were well ahead of them now, and all the two needed to do was stay out ahead.

The freight slowed after several miles, going up a long, even grade. Hatfield waved to the train crew before the sorrel took the lead.

It was late in the afternoon when they sighted Warwick, far off in the western distance. The approach to the town was partially screened by high mesquite growth and harsh buttes that thrust up from the dry, sandy soil. The sun was red as a ruby over the mountains before them. Their wide hats shaded their eyes, but they were blinking from the long spell of bright light and choked by the dust that was always in the air.

"Look, there's Vane!" exclaimed Hatfield.

The manager of the Star 8 was hitting down toward the town. The blue's stride was uneven.

"Picked up a stone, I reckon," growled Pete.

His companion began spurting out, urging the golden sorrel to run. Vane swung in his leather, his dark-mustached face twisting as he recognized his arch-foe. He began to beat the blue over the neck with his leaded quirt, digging his spurs deep into the lame mustang's gouged ribs.

At a breath-taking pace, Goldy gained on the blue. That night would fall suddenly, and Hatfield had to stop Vane from getting in ahead of him before it was dark. He drew a Colt, and low over the sorrel's neck, whispered him on.

Vane thought he could make it, but the sorrel's speed was too great. Fifty yards from the blue, Hatfield could see Vane's furious, red face as the chief of the Syndicate turned to shoot back at him.

The bullet flew wide, and Hatfield's Colt spat like an echo. Vane's hat flew off, the chin strap snapped by the bullet's force. Vane ducked, nearly lost his seat, grabbed for the horn with both hands. The blue lost his stride for a moment and the sorrel raced up. The Ranger shouted a command to halt.

Vane turned again, the pistol gripped in his hand. Hatfield let him have it, but he wasn't aiming to kill. As the Ranger's hogleg spoke, Vane whipped in twisted agony from his saddle, hung by a stirrup for an instant, then fell to the hot sand. The blue limped on.

Hatfield hit the dirt, darted to his prisoner, snatched the gun from his limp paw. Vane's black eyes were red with pain and baffled rage. But there was fear in them, too, for he had seen this big waddy in action too often. The chin strap drew up the Ranger's grim, rugged jaw and the gray-green eyes had an Arctic coldness to them. Heavy Colt in his long, thin hand, he stood over his prisoner.

Vane was no longer the dapper leader he had been. Blood stained his once-neat clothing — blood that had been drawn by Ranger lead. Dust and tears of pain marred his gear, streaked his face with dirt and powder-smoke.

"Don't — don't shoot, Harris!" he pleaded.

"Huh, I figgered yuh was yeller under that smooth, hard shell," sneered the big Ranger menacingly.

Panic streaked through the dark eyes. Hatfield had read his man right. As long as everything was going his way, George Vane was tough and strong. But the hombre who captured him had broken his nerve.

Pete Norris came spurring up, slapping

his mustang on the rump with his hand. He slid down and stood beside Hatfield, but he couldn't resist aiming a kick at Vane's ribs.

"Yuh made me plenty of trouble, blast yuh!" he snarled.

"Night's here," said the Ranger.

The sun had gone behind the western mountains. The blanket of dark fell over the land. Stars appeared with startling suddenness. Not yet had the moon gone beyond a bright glow on the horizon.

"Tie his hands, Pete," ordered the Ranger. "I reckon he can help us a lot when he starts squawkin'."

"Hang yuh!" cried Vane. "I won't talk." But as the tall man shifted threateningly toward him, Vane blurted: "Take me to the sheriff. I got a right to be formally arrested, Harris."

"Dry up," snapped Norris.

He was thinking of that terrible night when he had lost the Slash E bunch, of the stampede when he had had Miss Atchinson's life-saving herd taken, of what he had undergone in wounds and pain. He wasn't in a forgiving mood. Venomously he slapped the manager across the mouth.

"You'll get yours, both of you!" screamed Vane, shielding himself with his arms. "And damn quick!"

189

"I s'pose yuh mean Mohle," growled Hatfield, feeling for information.

Vane's jaw dropped, his black eyes rolled red.

"You devil!" he gasped. "How'd you know? Who told you?"

"I know plenty. Guire's hittin' tonight with a hundred and fifty men."

Vane gulped as his eyes fearfully searched the shadowed face of the tall man.

"Mohle's in Warwick. You was on yore way to report to him. He's yore chief. The Star Eight's been the outlet for the rustlin' all over Texas."

"Curse you, you can't beat us!" raged Vane. "Guire and Mohle will wipe your friends out!"

What Norris had told the Ranger, besides what he had overheard at the hidden rustler stronghold, crystallized to certainty as Vane, shaken and confused by the tall hombre's shrewdness and power, let the cat out of the bag. Hatfield knew that Guire actually meant to attack Warwick that evening.

"Shore," he mused. "They'll want to take them prisoners outa the jail, to prevent any squawkin'. And the chief ranchers of Brewster are in Warwick." He straightened up. "Gimme my spare gun, Pete. You can use Vane's. Hold 'em on him, shoot him dead if

190

he tries to escape. Fetch him to Peewee Cort's house."

"Where yuh goin'?"

"I better get right down to Warwick, fast as I can go. Vane, who is Mohle? There ain't any such hombre of that name that I savvy in Warwick."

But George Vane had got his second wind. He was plainly in awe and terror of his hidden chief. The Ranger figured he had extracted about as much information as he had time to force from the Star 8 boss. He straddled the waiting sorrel. With a wave to Norris, he swung at a gallop toward the blinking lights of Warwick.

An hour later he was on the main street, heading for the plaza. Lamps were shining from the warehouse in which the Brewster stockmen usually met.

"Holdin' another powwow, I reckon," he muttered.

There were some citizens on the awninged walks, and the saloons were open. As he came in from the southeast, the heavy thudding of hoofs pounded from the opposite direction. A long line of masked horsemen, led by a giant with flaming red hair visible under his notched Stetson, appeared between the buildings and headed for the jail.

Red Guire and his bunch were sweeping

191

in for the massacre! They came in at full-tilt, heavy guns ready for the scrap. More and more bunches of the notched-hatted devils, bandanna masks up to hide most of their features, rode low over their fresh rested mustangs. They surged out, spewing into Warwick for the kill.

They swept past the little jail, in which a lamp was burning up front. There Tad Durban held the six rustlers who had been taken at the western gulch. A dozen of Guire's men split off from the main body and headed for the lock-up.

The dust from the pounding hoofs rose high in the air. Jim Hatfield was cut off from the jail by the full forces of Red Frankie's killers. He saw them heading for the lighted meeting hall.

"Goin' to shoot 'em down in there," he grunted.

Colt flying into his hand, he spurted the sorrel to cut them off — one man alone against an army. He knew he must save the stockmen. Intent on their meeting, they would be easy prey for the killers of Red Frankie Guire and the hidden devil he knew only as Mohle.

The Ranger's Colt came up. At an angle Hatfield sped straight for the giant on the black stallion, out in front of his great array of gunnies.

"Guire!" he roared.

He fired an instant later, as the redheaded giant looked around and saw the streaking horseman.

"There he is — it's Harris, boys!" bellowed Guire.

But his shout became a thunder of cursing as the lead from the flaring Ranger's Colt cut through the flying black mustang's neck. The animal whirled around in midair, backbone doubling up so that his rider was shaken loose. The stallion shrieked in agony and fury at the wound. Guire couldn't hold him and the great beast left the line and came crow-hopping straight toward the tall Ranger.

Guire, swearing a blue streak, realized that his animal was hurt, uncontrollable, taking him right onto the guns of the big hombre he feared. He disengaged his huge boots from the tapped stirrups and landed running, gun coming up to pin Hatfield.

It was pointblank range as Red Frankie Guire, legs spread, crouched for fair aim and let go. Hatfield's Colt, concentrated on the red-headed chief of the gunnies, boomed a shade ahead of Guire's. Both bullets flew wide in the shack duel. The jolting speed of the golden sorrel, zigzagging with the rider's knee pressures, prevented both from making a quick hit.

Hatfield was carried on past. He whipped in his saddle and fired twice. As he turned the sorrel on a dime and Goldy pivoted, a full volley from the main band of killers *whooshed* with sickening deadliness through the space he had occupied an instant before.

Goldy saved the day. The Ranger had to shift his gun grip. The giant chief of the rustlers was thrusting his Colt up at the Ranger's body to blow him inside out. But the sorrel struck out with his left fore-hoof. The giant, hit in the belly, doubled up with a gasp of anguish, his wind knocked out. His bullet roared into the dirt under Goldy.

Before the falling rustler hit the ground, Hatfield snapped a shot into his head as the sorrel's speed checked an instant. The Ranger slug penetrated the top of Guire's cranium, driving deep in the evil brain.

Red Frankie was dead before he landed, a limp bundle of flesh and bone in the dust — vulture bait. . . .

A roar of rage rose in the masked throats of the killers. They swerved to concentrate on the man who had finished their infamous chief. Guns were rising to pin Hatfield.

He jerked his right rein, and the sorrel

obediently turned and flashed through a narrow aisle between buildings. The rustlers' bullets surged into the wood and dirt, their howls of disappointment ringing on the air. Goldy, urged by his tall master, streaked up Tin Can Alley toward the meeting hall.

Hatfield leaped to earth, ran toward the open window. The stockmen, Brant Tazewell and the rest, had heard the sudden gunfire. They were half-warned already by the Ranger's quick action.

"Gents, Guire's come in with a hundred and fifty rustlers to wipe yuh out!" bellowed Hatfield.

He dived through the window and landed inside. From the secret pocket in which snuggled the star on the silver circle — emblem of the Texas Rangers — he pulled his badge. They stared at it as he pinned it on his vest.

"A Ranger!" cried Tazewell.

"No time to talk now," snapped Hatfield, taking command. "Knock them lights out pronto and man the winders." Across the plaza heavy guns were barking. "They're after those prisoners at the jail. Get yore guns ready. Here comes the main bunch."

"Help! Help! Rustlers!"

The cry for aid came from the lock-up, Durban's quarters.

"That's Ben Walton callin'!" exclaimed Tazewell.

Chapter XIX
Mass Battle

There were sixty fighting men in the hall. The lights were quickly put out, and Hatfield scurried to the front door, peered out.

Guire's band were pulling themselves together after the death of their giant chief Red Frankie. They had swung up to carry out their orders. They meant to wipe out the ranchers of Brewster at the meeting that had been called to decide the fate of the six prisoners and further action to be taken against the cattle thieves.

Guns were still spitting red-yellow flashes in the darkness, at the jail across the plaza. The dust rose high. The killers, aware that the alarm was up, were howling with wolfish rage. The line of horsemen swept in. Colts began blaring, slugs driving into windows and the front door.

In reply the stockmen fired. The Ranger's accurate guns counted hardly a miss. Crouched to one side of the half-open door, he bobbed in and out to make his strikes.

A rustler, taken in the body by the law's lead, crashed under the driving hoofs of the hard-riding devils pouring past the warehouse. Another yipped with a smashed shoulder, fell out of line and rode off for the west.

Thick and fast, hundreds on hundreds of .45 slugs were exchanged. The stockmen, rising to fighting might behind the tall Ranger's cool example, handed out better than the two-to-one odds. In shelter, they could hold the masked killers back. Guire had thought to catch them unaware in a lighted hall, but Jim Hatfield's swift work had spoiled the terrible game, turned the massacre the other way.

Brant Tazewell, at the other side of the door, was shooting well. Olliphant, another big stockman, treasurer of the Union, covered a front window.

Lead came through, propelled by the rustler guns. Some of the men the Ranger sought to assist took it, but only two of them were hit mortally. The rest had flesh injuries in arm or shoulder.

Saddle after saddle emptied as the rustler line swung and came flying back, guns flashing death into the wooden building. Hatfield's pistols were hot in his slim hands, but his heart never speeded its steady beat. His brain was cool, in absolute control of the coordination of muscle and mind.

Guire's strategy, mapped out by Mohle, had been based upon the surprise element of getting the stockmen under their guns inside the lighted hall before the alarm came up. Hatfield had scotched this. Guire was dead. His lieutenants, picked off by the clever Ranger who could diagnose the formation of such bands, sought to rally the killers. But twenty-five of their number lay dead on the bare expanse of plaza and in the dust-clouded road. Another three dozen had felt the bitter lead of vengeful guns.

High courage was not in the make-up of such hyenas, who always needed the odds in their favor. The appalling pistols of Hatfield, the steady fire of his pals in the warehouse, cut them off short.

"There they go!" bawled Tazewell triumphantly.

The shattered army didn't come back again to the attack. They turned their lathered, fiery-eyed mustangs and streaked west for the chaparral, spurs dug in, crouched low over their horses.

Jim Hatfield, Colt in hand, ran out and kept shooting after them. But they had had a bellyful, and disappeared swiftly in the night.

Stunning silence descended over Warwick, after the banging reports of hundreds of pistols. Ear-drums began to shriek in the abrupt absence of gun reports.

Jim Hatfield whistled for the sorrel. Goldy, who had stayed in the alley to the rear out of harm's way, came trotting up to him.

Now the yells of citizens and the cries of alarmed women broke the moment of stillness after the fight. People began emerging from their hiding places, and the stockmen came streaming out to follow Hatfield.

"Hey — for Gawd's sake — this way!" a weak voice begged.

The dust still hung chokingly in the warm night air. Wounded men were groaning with the pain of their hurts. Hatfield, bleeding from half a dozen bullet nicks, turned the sorrel over toward the jail, from which the call for aid had come.

The light still burned inside. The door was wide open. Hatfield dismounted as someone called to him from the side. A man staggered toward him, wiping blood from his face.

"They hit us!" gasped Deputy Ben Walton. His right hand was torn and bleeding, and he held an empty gun in his left. "What's happened to Tad? Blast their dirty hides, the yeller skunks!"

He followed Hatfield into the office. Sheriff Tad Durban lay flat on his face, his bald head gleaming in the light. The bulky figure of the sheriff was quite still, with a big pool of blood spreading around his fat belly. His arms were extended and his fists clenched tight in death.

Walton knelt by his friend, cursing a blue streak against the men who had killed Durban. The Ranger glanced toward the iron-barred gate into the cells. It was open, unlocked by Durban's keys, which were still in the lock.

"I was walkin' over for a drink when they attacked," Walton said as Tazewell and the stockmen crowded in. "They hit the door and got pore Tad before he could draw."

The sheriff's guns were still in the holster, hanging from a wooden peg near his desk. Blood was flowing from Walton's gashed hand. He gritted his teeth as he held it tightly in his left.

"Emptied my gun at 'em. They nicked me."

Hatfield swung, knelt beside the dead man. The sheriff hadn't been any too bright, thought the Ranger, as he went over the body. Door unlocked, guns on a peg, taken unaware though he had six dangerous prisoners. The captives had easily been rescued by Guire's band as they retreated. All along Durban had made trouble for him, opposed him, going off half-cocked.

He rolled Durban over on his back, the limp arms falling sideward across the bulging stomach. Now he saw the bullet hole, blasted through the diaphragm and clear to the heart. His keen eyes took it all in, the black powder smudges on the shirt and the fishy-white skin. On the right hand, too, still clenched —

"He was shot with the gun pretty close against him," he said. "Look, Tazewell. What the devil's this in his fingers?"

He had opened the fingers and saw something glinting white in the lamplight. It had been clutched in the dead sheriff's hand.

Curiously he took it between thumb and forefinger, turned it over and over. It was an inch long but not straight, had a curlicue shape, and wasn't more than an eighth as wide. Save for the jagged end, which was darkened with blood, it was evenly beveled, with a widening spiral termination like a pearl cut in half.

"Huh," growled the Ranger. "It's a chunk of mother-of-pearl."

His swift brain picked up the clue. That sort of inlay was used to trim expensive six-shooters.

"Durban must've let the killer get close to him 'cause he had no idea of bein' attacked.

201

Then when he savvied his danger, he grabbed for the hogleg, got hold of it. There was a tussle, but the murderer turned the barrel and let go. . . ."

He broke off, turning to look up at the intent ranchers grouped about him.

"Walton," Hatfield growled, rising up, "let me see that fancy gun of yores."

Ben Walton wasn't present any longer.

"He jest slipped out, Ranger!" a man near the door said.

With a curse, the tall man sprang to the door. There were more citizens outside, but Ben Walton wasn't among them. He had left town, and had left fast.

"He wanted Durban's keys, I reckon, and the sheriff finally got wise," Hatfield decided. "They fought for the gun. That's how Walton's hand got cut, when the chunk of sharp inlay come out."

A bright light burst upon him as he deduced the shooting of the sheriff. Ben Walton had done it!

"Now I savvy why Durban always was ag'in me. He never had an idea of his own. Walton give 'em to him!" He faced the men, his wide mouth grim. "Gents, there's still a big passel of them rustlers loose, and they got their real chief leadin' 'em. I want volunteers to ride with me. I savvy where their hideout is. We got to clean 'em out. Every man who hones to fight with the Rangers, be ready with guns and a fresh horse in half an hour."

He swung on his heel, for he needed a drink and something to eat. Through his quick work, Hatfield knew he was on the right trail of Mohle, and he wanted to get the wired reply from Austin.

It was waiting for him. He roused the operator, who gave him the message from McDowell.

PHIL MOHLE HUNG BY ATCHINSON AND OTHER STOCKMEN TWENTY YEARS AGO STOP KNOWN AS KING OF THE RUSTLERS STOP LUCK McDOWELL

The tall Ranger crumpled the paper in his hand. He was still puzzled.

As he stalked over toward Peewee Cort's, he saw Sue Atchinson run across the plaza and throw herself into Pete Norris' arms. George Vane, wounded and sadly bedraggled, was trussed up. Norris had fetched him in.

"I thought they'd killed you!" the young woman was crying.

Pete couldn't be bothered to talk much.

He grinned as he kissed her.

"Jim saved me," he said.

Hatfield seized Vane and shoved him inside the mayor's lighted home. Peewee, still suffering from his wound, sat propped in an armchair. The shock and injury had sent him downhill, for he was well along in years.

"Nice work, Ranger," quavered Cort, his old eyes lighting. "Bill McDowell couldn'ta done it better in his younger days."

"That's a mighty fine compliment, Cort," Hatfield said gravely. "But I ain't done yet. I'm on the trail of a sidewinder named Mohle, who's chief of this bull rustler set-up. King of the Rustlers, they call him."

"Huh? Why, I was with Pop Atchinson when we strung Mohle up, twenty years ago last April Fool's Day!"

"There's another one loose, then. Did he have any relations with the same handle?"

"No — oh, yeah, wait now! I remember!"

It was a long time back, and Cort's face screwed up.

"Yeah, Ranger. Phil Mohle had a younger brother, Ken. He was only a scrawny yearling, though, not more'n sixteen at the time. We captured him with Phil, who was leader of a killer gang in these parts. Ken Mohle bein' so young, we let him go. But Atchinson figgered he needed some punishment and warnin'. He took one of the cattle thieves' irons, heated her up and branded Ken with a big 'R' right on the back. I still remember how he yelped."

Cort grinned at the recollection.

"Would yuh know Ken Mohle if yuh saw him now?" asked Hatfield. "How about this here Ben Walton, Durban's deputy? Does he look like Mohle?"

Peewee Cort shrugged. "It was a hell of a long time ago. Ben Walton's forty pounds heavier than that shank-legged kid. I only seen Ken Mohle a couple times. Walton's face is bearded, too, and his hair's lighter. The years'd change him so his own maw wouldn't savvy him, though I reckon Walton could be Mohle."

Men were collecting in the plaza, with fresh mustangs and shotguns, rifles and Colts, ready to ride under the command of the great Texas Ranger. Jim Hatfield's name was being spoken about the town with awe and admiration. They realized that single-handed he had uncovered the great rustler ring which had so long terrorized the State.

Hatfield swung to the front door. George Vane, in a dither of alarm, hands tied, had been listening to the talk. Scowling, threatening stockmen were on the veranda, standing in a menacing knot. Mention of a long rope was being bandied about as Vane's perfidy became clear.

The Ranger towered over the captive, gray-green eyes cold on him.

"What d'yuh say, Vane?" he growled. "The jig's up. Ben Walton is Ken Mohle, come back to get revenge and make hisself a big fortune as king of the rustlers. He knowed of that secret tunnel his brother Phil used to run cows through. I know where the hideout on the Circle Three range is. Yuh wanted Atchinson's spread as a depot for stock run from all parts of the Trans-Pecos. Yore part's clear. You was the front, with yore Star Eight, to market the stolen stock."

"Curse you, Ranger!" whimpered Vane, licking his thin lips. "You're a devil!"

Hatfield grasped his shoulder, pulled him to his feet, shoved him out on the porch. The dead rustlers who had been strewn over the plaza and in the streets had been picked up and laid out in an even line, body to body. Vane stared at the corpses, eyes widening.

"C'mon, let's use that handy beam on him, boys," somebody cried. "He's a traitor, posin' as a decent rancher and ruinin' us all!"

"I'll do anything you say, Ranger!" Vane

shrilled.

Instinctively he shrank back toward the tall man. He knew Hatfield was the only man who could keep them from stringing him up.

"Been a lotta folks damaged by yore thievin', Vane," Hatfield said. "Yuh can help make it up. How many cows runnin' yore spread now?"

Vane pondered. "Around twenty thousand, I suppose. We shipped pretty regularly."

"And how about that safe in yore office? Got the cash in it yuh received for the stolen stock?"

"Expenses run high, Ranger. We had a lot of men to pay off. Still, there's plenty in there."

"We're all set, Ranger, when yuh want us!" Brant Tazewell sang out.

The fighting men of Brewster were itching to start on the trail of the cattle thieves.

Chapter XX
Rustler Hideout

Jim Hatfield had but a dozen picked men behind him as he rode the golden sorrel at a swift clip through the warmth of the Texas afternoon. They were pushing their horses up the east line of the Comanches. The brazen sun beat upon their bodies, drinking greedily the moisture from their skins.

Brant Tazewell, president of the Brewster Stockmen, Cimarron Jones and stout John Olliphant, all import ranchers of Texas, and several waddies of proved fighting ability, rode with the tall Ranger. They paused for a bite and a drink, glad to stretch their limbs. Hatfield rode over toward a bunch of steers in a draw. Goldy drove one of the animals back. Close to the group of squatted men, in the shade of a high mesquite clump, Hatfield roped and threw the beast.

"Star Eight brand, gents," he said, indicating the foot-high brand on the dusty flank of the bawling steer. "Take a good look."

All of them were experts. Tazewell especially knew every brand in the book in Texas.

"Looks perfect," he growled.

The Ranger butchered the steer efficiently and quickly. He set to work with a skinning knife and in record time the hide was off the dead animal. He flattened out the hide, inside out, so that the brand could be seen from the other side.

"Circle Three, shore enough," agreed Tazewell. The others nodded confirmation. "Them rewrite men's good. Yuh gotta give 'em credit."

"Too good to let run loose," growled Ol-liphant.

From the inside, the old brand stood out clearly from the fresh. The inner hide couldn't be blotted. It was, however, an expensive way of proving ownership. The Ranger had butchered one steer just to cinch the evidence.

"Yuh can divvy up accordin' to proven losses, gents," he remarked as they prepared to head on. "There oughta be some salvage, anyway."

Groups of dust-covered, sullen-faced cattle thieves drifted back to the hide-out in the Comanches west of the high peaks. Many carried Ranger and stockmen's lead or the bleeding gashes, taken in the wild fight at Warwick.

Split up according to the worth of their mustangs, they were coming in, miles apart. Forced to stop for water and to give their winded horses brief respite, they turned their spur-gouged, lathered and puffing mounts into the corral below and staggered stiff-legged to find liquor and food.

Here they felt safe, behind guarded trails to the west, the foothills covered with dense chaparral and pine forests. Sentries were always posted on the heights that way. And eastward they had the unknown pass through the Comanches.

It was getting late, the sun reddening in the west. Men were lounging about, tearing at cold beef strips, taking swigs of whisky to wash it down.

A big hombre in black leather and double-notched hat, with bluish beard stubble on his horse-face, finally swallowed his last bite. He took a long drink of liquor from a bottle and tossed it back into the rocks.

He rose, sweeping them with hard eyes. Everybody knew "Black Ed" McCrory, Guire's right-hand man in the brand-switching game. Black Ed had rustled cows from the Mexican haciendas in Sonora to the Canadian border, and his ability to rewrite a brand amounted to evil genius.

"Okay, boys," he began, voice deep and gruff. "Mohle ain't in, so I'm takin' charge. Savvy?"

Nobody made any objection. They waited to hear what Black Ed had to tell them. Most of them were sullen, and what McCrory went on to say suited them fine.

"That big jigger is a Texas Ranger, boys. I glimpsed his star. I ain't foolin' with such, not with a hombre like that. He well nigh smashed us complete in Warwick. He was waitin' for us. Frankie Guire's dead, and so's Francisco, to say nothin' of Rooster Sprague and three dozen more men of ours. I don't aim to be next."

"Me neither," someone snarled, and the chorus was complete.

"I'm takin' to the tall timber, 'cause I figger these parts ain't healthy," continued McCrory. "There's plenty of spreads up north, where the Rangers don't ride, outside the State. And I'm startin' soon as I've had a coupla hours' snooze."

"How about Mohle?" asked another rustler.

"He can foller if he wants to. If he'd rather, he can stay and play with that big jigger."

They were all in agreement that the game was up. After a short sleep, they would split and ride off.

As Black Ed McCrory turned away, a hoot came from the western ridge. The cattle thieves tensed, hairy hands stealing to gun butts. Presently a wild-eyed sentry came running down to the bluff overlooking the camp.

"Hey, they're comin' — eighty or ninety armed possemen from Warwick! George Vane's with 'em, and he's pointin' the way through the secret trails!"

Pandemonium ensued. These hombres

had had a stomachful of fighting. They had seen their leaders knocked off by Ranger lead. Having decided to depart, they were in no mood to stand and fight it out.

Black Ed led the exodus. He ran with bowlegged stride mustang, slapped on the saddle, cinched up and leaped aboard. He cut down across the creek and headed for the horse corral. With his rope he got himself a fresh tunnel pass.

Gunshots began to crack up above, from the west, as the avenging stockmen swiftly came up on the rustler hideout. The hundred cattle thieves were decamping, however. They streamed down for the secret pass, which they could block to hold back the pursuit, once they were through.

Up over the ridge came Pete Norris, in the lead of the waddies and fighting men collected in Warwick for the attack on the rustler stronghold. Rifle in hand, Norris urged his gunfighters to hustle on. Only an hour remained of daylight in which to make good the capture.

A long line of grim-faced Texans burst into view above the camp. Shots cracked in the hills, echoing up and down between the steep walls of the Comanches. The attackers swarmed down into the camp.

It was empty now of rustlers. They had

crossed the creek and were plunging into the dense bush to the east, evidently swallowed up in the frowning, sheer battlements of the mountain peaks.

Through the dank tunnel, the sound of the running stream echoing hollowly, Black Ed McCrory rode his mustang at the head of the pushing, retreating rustlers. He knew the way by heart.

The faint streaks of light faded as he reached the middle of the long underground pass. He had helped run thousands on thousands of steers through here, to turn them out on the Star 8 range. From there Vane's cowboys had picked them up, loaded them into cattle cars and run them to market.

McCrory had no worries about escaping the clutches of the law. Before Pete Norris and his men could trail them through, the thieves would all be out. Big rocks had long ago been set, ready to close the pass at either end.

He spurted ahead, as he saw the splotch of daylight at the eastern end of the tunnel, reached the turn and made it. A curse spat from his harsh lips as he suddenly jerked his reins, pulling his hairy mustang back on its haunches.

In the narrow trail, just outside the mouth

of the tunnel, big rocks had fallen. They had been pushed over from hair-trigger sets on the side ledges.

A Winchester muzzle rose to cover his breast and a cold, dread voice called out to him.

"Reach!"

"The Ranger!" gasped McCrory.

He knew that hangman's nooses awaited him in a dozen States, making surrender impossible. He could not spur ahead, because the rocks were held by Jim Hatfield, a dozen crack shots, Brant Tazewell and the other ranchers.

Without hesitation he sacrificed his bronc. He reared the animal up with a swift jerk of the reins and slid down the beast's rump. At the same instant the Winchester and two other rifles cracked and the bullets thudded into the horse. But its bulk protected McCrory for the needed instants as he scrabbled back around the rocky turn.

Hatfield's second shot cut a chunk from Black Ed's calf as he made it, legs drawing in after him. McCrory felt the tearing lead, the hot blood spurting from the wound. A couple of hurrying cattle thieves nearly ran over him. Wide-eyed and swearing sulphurously, he scrambled to his boots and limped back.

"Blocked, yuh can't get through!" growled McCrory. "That Ranger jigger's on the other side!"

Mad curses rose at this sad news.

"C'mon. We gotta try to shoot it out on the other side, before they get down."

Swiftly they turned, but others were crushing after them, and the tunnel was narrow. Horses had to be turned. Yells echoed in the long pass, confusion and fear streaking through the black hearts of the killers. But at last they made it. The van spewed from the western end of the secret tunnel.

Pete Norris stuck his head up from behind a rock.

"Throw down yore guns, blast yuh!" he bellowed, rifle up.

A rustler threw a bullet his way. It spat chunks of granite into Norris' face. The rifle replied and the hombre left his horse, crashing dead with a slug between the eyes.

Instantly the rest of Pete's crew opened up with a volley from the semi-circle he had swiftly formed around the tunnel exit. He was carrying out Hatfield's orders to the letter. Assisted by the broken Vane, who pointed out the way, Norris had rushed his fighters into position with dispatch, cutting off retreat.

Hot and heavy the exchange of lead went

215

on. Half a dozen desperate killers made a dash for it, seeking to turn north out of the constricted pass and run for it. Not one made more than a hundred yards before being brought down by the deadly rancher guns.

"Never get past that big line," growled Black Ed, back in the tunnel. "We'll wait till dark and then try to make a run for it, boys."

The trapped thieves had but an hour to wait. The firing died off. The rustlers in the pass, crouched hidden, gathering strength for their last attempt at freedom.

A cold, clammy wind blew from the eastern gap of the tunnel. Somebody's teeth rattled in the chill gloom.

"Cut that out," snarled Black Ed. "I'll shoot the first man who makes a dash to give up."

The silence, the waiting, made the moments drag like hours. Suddenly a man coughed and another sneezed.

"I smell smoke," a killer complained.

Everybody did. Like rats caught in a blocked hole, they began coughing, eyes burning as acrid woodsmoke drifted through, sucked in by the breeze. It grew worse and worse.

"I — I can't stand no more," strangled a man in despair.

The mustangs were shifting restlessly, terrified by the smoke. The men had to fight them to hold them down. Clouds of acrid smoke enveloped them.

"Blast that dirty Ranger," coughed Black Ed. "He's burnin' cowhide now!"

Retching, unable to bear it any longer, the trapped cattle thieves surged out into the light. Half of them started their guns going, shooting at the grim stockmen covering them from the ring of rocks.

Bullets tore back at them, picking them off as they sought to make a mad dash for safety. Crowding one another to get mounted and started, the rustlers felt the burning lead of retribution from those they had ravaged. Gunny after gunny, cursing and shooting, crashed from his saddle.

The smoke was thinner now as it curled from the tunnel mouth. A tall man, two Colts up and going full-blast, suddenly burst from the vapor, catching the killers in the rear. Behind him came Brant Tazewell and the bunch Jim Hatfield had had with him.

"Throw down, rustlers!" the Ranger bellowed over the crashing din.

All hope of escape deserted them. Rustlers began tossing their weapons away, raising their hands high over their Stetsons. The appearance of the Ranger had convinced them that they were through. A few kept shooting, knowing that only death awaited them at the hands of the law.

"Get over to the south and stand quiet, those who quit," they heard Jim Hatfield roar.

Crouched by a huge red boulder near the tunnel mouth, the Ranger aimed for the fleeing individuals who sought escape. One by one the accurate Colts brought the running gunnies to earth, abetted by the fire of Norris and his force.

Then the fight was over. Prisoners in droves stood quiet, disarmed, ready to take their medicine. The final shot broke, rattled in the deep Comanches. The smoke of burnt powder wafted up against the frowning red battlements of the mountains.

Jim Hatfield, face grim but filled with satisfied triumph, lined the captives up and walked along them. He paused in front of Black Ed McCrory, who scowled into the gray-green eyes.

"Where's Ken Mohle?" Hatfield demanded.

McCrory spat. "Ain't seen him, Ranger. Can I roll me a quirly?"

Hatfield nodded, went on. Nobody knew anything about Mohle. The prisoners were being secured by the ranchers. Hatfield left the clean-up to Brant Tazewell, climbed up to the point where George Vane, held by a couple of cowmen, was sitting on a flat rock.

"Did Mohle savvy the combination of that Star Eight safe?" he inquired.

Vane nodded. "He and I were the only ones who knew it."

CHAPTER XXI
LAST SHOT

On the golden sorrel, the tall Ranger was far ahead of the following stockmen. Six of them had accompanied him as he headed in for the buildings of the Star 8. Goldy, however, had outdistanced their mounts.

Alert and ready for trouble in the night, Hatfield saw that the ranch was unlighted. He dismounted a safe distance out, then came sneaking in, a Colt in one hand. But the Star 8 was deserted. No one challenged him. No shots came blasting out.

He rounded the great house to the office. The outer door stood half-open, and he slipped inside. The fire hadn't gone far. It had been checked near the door.

In the corner he struck a match, shading it with his big slim hand. The square safe was open, the inside panel as well, its drawers pulled out.

"He made it," he growled.

Checking up to be certain there were no hiding drygulchers in the place, he came to the room in which Pete Norris had been held prisoner. When he heard sounds of stirring inside, he threw up his Colt. He set his lantern, with which he had lit the way, on the floor.

"Come out with yore hands up," he called.

"Hey, mister, help us! We can't move. We're tied up!"

Hatfield kicked the door in, sprang to one side. The lantern cast its yellow rays inside. Half a dozen figures lay on the boards, hands and ankles bound tightly with rawhide cords.

He stepped in, curiously looking them over. They were Vane's handful, left at the ranch when the boss of the spread rode for Warwick. Ken Mohle wasn't among them. They turned helpless eyes upon him, saw the silver star on the silver circle.

"Yuh're a Ranger!" one of them gasped. "Mighta known it!"

"Where's Mohle?" demanded Hatfield.

"Curse his hide," snarled the waddy, "he done this to us! The jig was up. We knowed that. He come here and opened the safe to get all the cash there was in it. We asked for our share. But he stuck guns on us, made me tie up the others. Then he roped me. He rode off two hours ago."

"Which way?"

The hombre was glad to draw the noose around Mohle's neck.

"North, far as I could hear his hoss's hoofs."

"There'll be men along soon to loose yuh," the Ranger told them. "I'm ridin'."

He raced outside, hunted for the fresh trail leading north. Squatting close to it, the lantern held for light, he checked on it so he could recognize it again.

Then he whistled for the sorrel, and Goldy trotted up.

The red dawn came up over the barren expanses of Pecos County, up at the north end of the wild Comanches.

"There he is, Goldy," the Ranger growled. His eyes were on the faint hoof-marks in the shifting, sandy dirt. "We guessed right. He's on his way to cross the Pecos at Horse-head."

Pausing only to check the sign by striking matches in the night, he had relentlessly pursued Ken Mohle. The king of the rustlers was fleeing with the wad of money from the sale of the stolen steer herds of Texas.

Mohle had stopped for an hour at a muddy waterhole, to refresh his mount and himself. The horse he rode, Hatfield knew before he even sighted them, was black and threw its left hind leg in a long stride. This he had deduced from the sign picked up. The faint dust ahead told him that Goldy's supremacy as a runner was still unchallenged in Texas. The sorrel, steady gait swiftly tearing off the miles, had come up close to the black.

As the sun rose over the wilderness, the tall Ranger shoved doggedly on, the wind of speed flapping the broad brim of his strapped Stetson.

Mohle sighted him from a rise as he looked back. The sun, now yellow in the brazen sky, glinted on metal from the king of the rustlers' gun.

Hatfield saw the smoke puff and heard the bullet *zing* off to the right. Colt in hand, he let the sorrel draw up, foot by foot, on the hard-riding Mohle. The king of cattle thieves was gouging and quirting his black mustang to give its last ounce of speed.

Mohle cast another look back. Mohle, alias Ben Walton, was the chow house keeper who, as deputy sheriff to the dull-witted Durban, had shaped the law's policy in Brewster County.

"A right smart sidewinder," thought Hatfield, his wide mouth set grimly, the dust sticking to his rugged, bronzed face.

With hidden skill, the outlaw had used Tad Durban for his own purposes, the power of suggestion making the sheriff a tool in his clever hands.

Mohle fired back again. This time the bullet spurted up dust a yard from the clapping hoofs of the flying sorrel. Hatfield held his lead. He crooned to the handsome gelding, his partner in the great rides they had made.

"Show that black what runnin' is," he urged.

A final burst of power brought the sorrel up within a hundred yards of the hard-pressed king of the rustlers. Mohle's eyes were glaring with red fury, the hard desperation of his kind reaching its acme in the terrible spoiler of the Texas ranges. He fired, teeth gritted as he jounced with the black's loping motion.

A slug bit a chunk from Hatfield's Stetson crown. Another one sliced a bit of flesh from his left forearm.

"Steady, Goldy," he murmured, cool and unhurried.

The Ranger Colt slowly rose, and the sweated shine of Mohle's face was a good target. For the first time the Ranger let go, thumb rising from the hammer. The firing-pin drove into the rim of the cartridge, exploding the powder which sent the .45 slug on its way.

Mohle suddenly twisted to the front. For an instant the murderous hombre rode straight on, erect in the saddle. Then as the black swerved to avoid a bunch of mesquite, the figure in the leather toppled off, crashed heavily, rolling on jagged rocks before coming to a halt.

A few moments later Hatfield, Colt up and ready in case Mohle was playing 'possum, reached the scene and reined in. He stared down at the king of the rustlers, whose shirt had been ripped by the sharp rock edges on which he had been thrown.

Mohle lay on his back, neck stretched and twisted to one side. There was a bluish bullet hole between the cold, fishy blue eyes of the king of the rustlers. He had been dead before he hit.

Hatfield turned him over on his face with his spurred boot. The sweated shirt, torn from the body by the sharp stones, hung in ribbons, exposing the ripped and bloody flesh.

A six-inch high "R" had been branded on his back twenty years before by Pop Atchinson. It was still plainly visible.

"I was right," grunted Hatfield.

Mohle had two pearl-trimmed guns. The Ranger took the bit of inlay he had removed from the dead Durban's hand. It fitted exactly. He rode over to rope the black, which had finally stopped running and put down its head to graze.

When Mohle's big, limp body was slung and tied on the mustang, the Ranger swung back for the Star 8 and Warwick.

Captain Bill McDowell banged the desk so furiously that the inkwell jumped.

"The cattle business is the life blood of Texas, Jim! Yuh've shore done a noble job."

Back at Headquarters, Hatfield was reporting in terse language the general effects of his trip to Brewster.

"This Mohle skunk," he said, "took the name 'King of the Rustlers,' after an older brother of his, who was hung by Atchinson and his vigilantes twenty years ago. Knowing of a secret pass between the Comanches, Cap'n, was mighty useful in disposin' of stolen stock. He was an expert brand-blotter and had picked up a bunch of other rewrite men. They chose that Star Eight 'cause it was easy to blotch the Circle Three to it, though them wolves could fix anything to pass inspection. Mohle aimed at gettin' plenty of money at wholesale rustlin', and on the side figgered on revenge. He killed Atchinson and tried to take over the Circle Three."

"But he didn't succeed. Yuh say this Vane give yuh help in the roundup."

"Yeah. He spilled the beans, once I got on the trail. Vane filled in the blanks for me. He's doin' all he can to make up for what he done."

"Sue's okay?"

"Shore. She'll salvage enough from the Star Eight cows and the cash Mohle tried to steal, so her and her new husband can make a go of it."

"Husband? She's hitched up?"

"Yeah. Her and that Pete Norris, of the Slash E, got married before I left Warwick."

Hatfield watched the face of his chief soften. McDowell cleared his throat and then got businesslike again. He rattled the report he picked up from the desk. "The Rio," he said gruffly. "Ain't a minute's peace."

Hatfield held out his slim hand. He read the sheriff's report of tense trouble to the south.

"There ain't now," he stated. "But there

will be. Runnin' out killers like Mohle helps some."

Outside, the golden sorrel waited. Hatfield came out and sprang into saddle.

They headed for the Rio, carrying with them Ranger law to the far reaches of the Lone Star State.

We hope you have enjoyed this Large Print book. Other Thorndike, Wheeler, Kennebec, and Chivers Press Large Print books are available at your library or directly from the publishers.

For information about current and upcoming titles, please call or write, without obligation, to:

Publisher
Thorndike Press
295 Kennedy Memorial Drive
Waterville, ME 04901
Tel. (800) 223-1244

or visit our Web site at:

http://gale.cengage.com/thorndike

OR

Chivers Large Print
published by AudioGO Ltd
St James House, The Square
Lower Bristol Road
Bath BA2 3BH
England
Tel. +44(0) 800 136919
info@audiogo.co.uk
www.audiogo.co.uk

All our Large Print titles are designed for easy reading, and all our books are made to last.